THE MORTUARY
MONSTER

By Andrew J. Stone

Chad,
Thanks so much for coming out
and the support. You rock! And
best of luck @ Stokercon!

Edited by
John Bruni

— aj stone

Published by StrangeHouse Books
(Strangehouse Books is an imprint of Rooster Republic Press LLC)

Copyright 2016 © Andrew J. Stone
Cover by Luke Spooner
www.carrionhouse.com

www.strangehouseonline.com

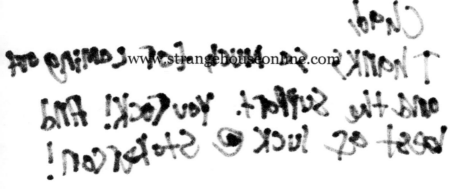

Chad!
Thanks for grabbing one & coming out and the suffer. You rock! And best of luck @ Stokercon!

THE MORTUARY MONSTER

ANDREW J. STONE

Acknowledgements

Without the following friends and all their wonderful advice, this book would not exist. So I owe a great deal of thanks to:

Geoff Nicholson, Jon Wagner, Caitlin Thomson, Ben Sneyd, Stephanie Taglianetti, Matthew Seidman, Tim Day, Lauren Artiles, Kim Bredberg, Garrett Cook, Pegi Stone, Cade Quinn, Cameron Pierce, and Matias Viegener.

For Lindsey, without whom, none of this would be possible.

THE DELIVERY

Gonzalo stares at the corpse as the first folds of flesh crawl through the crack. He takes hold of her skinless knees, spreading them farther apart, commanding the dead woman to push. As the baby's forehead burrows itself into the light, passing itself into life, Gonzalo screams.

The baby's flesh is covered in mold passed on from cadaverous mother to child. The corpse asks if the baby is out, and Gonzalo tells her it is. She asks if it's a boy or a girl, and after a quick inspection Gonzalo informs her it's a he. The corpse smiles a skeletal grin and lays her head back on the grass. Gonzalo wraps a towel around the boy, gently removing the mold, using the mixture of their tears as a cleaning fluid. Once the mold is gone he brings the boy's forehead to his lips and gives him a soft kiss. "Frank," he whispers. He says the name again as his thoughts press him into the past.

Gonzalo is in the cemetery. He is seven years old. Plaid socks are pulled up to his shins, and his black shorts cut off just before the knees. His shirt, also black, is missing two buttons around his belly which will be sunburnt badly, a discovery he will make with whimpers later in the evening. But for now he skips with a swagger that only the nearly dead possess who are so drunk off of pain that passing

9

becomes the only gift to live for. Gonzalo's pleasure is less lethal. For him it is simply break, the only time of day he is free of his family. For that he skips, taking in the scent of freshly cut grass and dodging the tombstones protruding from the earth. He has exactly fifteen minutes before his mother's whistle will ring, alerting him and his two sisters that they must immediately return to the mortuary for math. Gonzalo hates math almost as much as he hates his sisters, but his mind is far from psychological pain at the moment. After all he has fifteen minutes of freedom, almost a lifetime to Gonzalo. And with these fifteen minutes he will venture out to the far side of the cemetery, to the gravesite of a Mr. Frank Arthur Oatsplash (1800-1888) with whom he will converse about his masterpiece which, at the moment, looks like nothing so much as different shades of colored light randomly splashed across a coffin wood canvas. But when he arrives at the site Mr. Oatsplash is crying. Gonzalo reaches his hand out to comfort the old corpse, but the man brushes it off.

"What's wrong?" Gonzalo asks.

Without looking up Mr. Oatsplash says, "You have broken your promise."

Gonzalo giggles at the decrepit corpse. He tells him it's all right, that there's no need to cry. "Mr. Oatsplash," he says, "I would never break my promise because I never ever want to have a baby."

Then the boy gets serious, says, "I will never place another person in a position similar to mine or yours, Mr. Oatsplash. Never ever." But Mr. Oatsplash just shakes his head, tells the boy that he's lying. Gonzalo, now crying himself, pleads that he'd never have a baby because a baby would make him a parent, and his parents are even worse than his sisters.

"Please believe," he says. Mr. Oatsplash stops

crying, stops shaking when the boy places an arm on his shoulder. "I promise," Gonzalo says again, confident that his message is getting through.

Mr. Oatsplash lifts his head and looks into the boy's eyes. "You're a liar."

Beneath the light of the moon Gonzalo resumes whispering to his son. Between repeating the boy's name and unheard apologies to Mr. Oatsplash, Gonzalo gathers the courage to make another promise to another Frank. He says to his son in near silence, "I will get you out of this place."

PART ONE
BEFORE THE BIRTH

THE CADAVER TEA PARTY

Gonzalo has just finished his fourth Long Island, and it hasn't done a damn thing to lift his spirits. Not that this mood is unusual for Gonzalo; he spends most of his time these days sulking around the shadows of the cemetery, avoiding corpses as if it were his occupation. The man has been far removed from himself ever since his last attempt to leave this land, and his insides are starting to shine. But that was years ago, and Gonzalo has never before been so glum during the day of the Cadaver Tea Party. If asked before, any of the corpses would have said the annual get together is what keeps Gonzalo going, but now they aren't so sure. The mood of the party has followed Gonzalo's lead—silent and sullen. The tone at the table is timid and violent.

Gonzalo places the empty glass beside the other three. He says to the corpse on his right, "Get me another fucking drink, Fiona." And knocks his knuckles against the wood as he waits. Fiona stretches across the table, grabs the teapot—which she had filled with the liquored tea prior to the party —and pours Gonzalo another drink.

"To the next round." She clinks her glass against his before resting it against her mandible, tilting back her skull. The other four corpses at the table silently chew on crumpets in between sips.

As the tea taints Gonzalo's throat, his mind moves through hours until it reaches the afternoon, replaying his prior engagement with a Mr. and Mrs. Gunther as they sadly sauntered in the direction of his funeral parlor. The man let the woman in, and the bell above the door chimed, sending a shock through Gonzalo's stiff body, confirming the reality of his vision. "Hello," Gonzalo said coldly, squinting his eyes, trying to make out his sun-blocked visitors from the shadows. Besides the deliveryman, he hadn't seen a breathing human in many months.

"How do you do?" the man said, staying strong if only for the missus. The man extended his hand but Gonzalo didn't return the gesture. Forced to withdraw, the man said, "I'm Charles, and this here is my wife Ellen."

"Hell . . . Hello," Ellen said, sounding like death. And again, Gonzalo left them in the dark.

Minutes passed. The visitors were steeped in sadness. At one point Ellen looked to her husband. "Where's Hank? Where's our son?" Charles just shook his head, stunned.

All the while Gonzalo stood and stared, waiting for his vision to adjust, waiting for his guests to prove their authenticity against the shadows. Gonzalo placed a cigar in his mouth, lit it and inhaled. As the smoke from his exhalation permeated the room, he was able to separate the real from the irreal, the guests from the gone. Finally he said, "Welcome, friends."

Silence. The only sounds came from the missus as she shifted her weight from one foot to the other, causing the floorboards to creak. Gonzalo blinked continually as if realization had finally dawned, and he said to his guests, "Yes, so how may I be of assistance?"

Charles coughed his throat clear. "We need to

setup funeral arrangements."

"Naturally, but for whom?"

"Our son." Charles choked on each syllable as it surpassed his lips.

"And what is our newest guest's name?" Gonzalo said, giddy.

"Ha . . . Hank," Charles said.

"Hank, we had one of those once in the old days. Goddamn son of a bitch he was." Gonzalo shook the memory out of his brain and, feeling renewed, said, "With any luck you and the missus might be joining your son soon. Now wouldn't that be cause for party?"

"Pardon?" Charles said.

"Have you looked in a mirror lately? You're more ghastly than a ghost. And, well, last man I've seen so translucent, it wasn't a few hours till he met his match, and you know what did him in? Fellow finally saw his reflection in a mirror. The man was so pale he saw straight through to his heart, even witnessed its last beat before it stopped." Gonzalo let light laughter linger from his lips into the atmosphere. "Say, better get you a mirror old timer."

"For the love of God," the man uttered as his wife let loose a short screech.

"So do tell," Gonzalo went on, "How'd your son do it?" He paused, his face lit up. "Was it a gun wound? Poison? Accidental strangulation due to autoerotic asphyxiation?"

Ellen's eyes wetted her cheeks with salt water. Her man said, "Listen, sir, if my parents weren't buried here, and their parents, and the folks before theirs, I would kick your ass so hard it'd never see this cemetery again."

"If only you could, Charles. God, what a blessing that would be. But we digress. Give me a date. When can we get this goddamn thing over with?"

"Excuse me?" Charles said.

17

"You guys think you're so special, coming and going as you please. Must be nice to live among the living, to know a normal life. And you even play this sad act as you approach, and to what end? Well, I got news for you." Foam licked Gonzalo's lips. "Nothing can worsen my misery. Now, what day can we bury your boy, and when will he join my nightmare?"

"What the fuck is wrong with you?" Charles said, rolling back his sleeve.

"Please," Ellen said to her husband, barely audible above the shadows. "Not now. Think of Hank, dearie." She placed her hand on her husband's arm, visually cooling him. "Now," she said to Gonzalo, "we are free three days from now at six in the evening. We will see you then, Mr. Gonzalo. Good day."

Gonzalo wrote down the time and date, shaking his head at the audacity of his guests to wish him a goddamn good day. Before he looked up again, the bell above the door rang, signaling the silence to come.

Gonzalo wasn't surprised to find his cheeks lined with tears of his own. As Mr. and Mrs. Gunther left he saw himself seven years earlier, closing up the last coffin of his cemetery for good, preparing for his voyage into the void, that strange new place— society. His briefcase was full of clothes and his spirit was full of hope that had been so long suppressed, finally setting sail into the unknown again. Gonzalo had imagined he would soon be standing on green grass enclosed by a white picket fence, waving at neighbors walking by with a baseball glove hiding his hand. Instead another tear struck his cheek as the first stranger he came across shrieked, "What's wrong with you?"

Again, now, he hears Fiona say, "Gonzalo, what's wrong?"

Gonzalo shakes his head, lowering the empty glass to the table alongside the others. "Nothing," he says, extending his hand for hers. "Just another drink, if you will."

Fiona leaves the table to retrieve another teapot from the funeral parlor. When she returns to the patio she pours Gonzalo another drink and he quickly pulls it toward his lips. This time the tea hits his throat harshly, and as it swims into his stomach the liquor breaches his blood.

"So, Gonzalo," Fiona says, patting the corpse beside her. "Lionel was just telling us that you are an artist. Right, Lionel? Tell him what you just told us when Gonzalo here had gone into his mind."

"Well, I was saying," Lionel begins, but Gonzalo takes another sip of tea, and his mind is free in thought. He replays his interactions with the Gunthers once more, but unlike before, this time he plays the reel in his mind with hope. Yes, he thinks, and then mouths, "An opportunity!"

"A what?" Lionel says.

"Never mind that," Gonzalo says. "Go on."

"I just finished," Lionel says.

"And?" Gonzalo has lifted the drink to his lips again, trying to jog his memory with tea but to no avail.

After a moment's pause, Lionel says, "And how old is the artwork on the closed side of the cemetery? The canvases bear your signature, but I believed that side of the cemetery had been dead for ages."

"It has," Gonzalo lies. "Long before I came into being."

"Well, are you the artist?"

"Of course. When I was a boy I used to hang out on that side of the cemetery to find peace so I could create my craft."

"Ah," Fiona says. "A true artist breathes among

us."

"I didn't know you could paint," Victoria, who sits to Gonzalo's left, says. "What kind of painter are you?"

"I'm a Projectionist," Gonzalo says absent-mindedly.

"Yes," Lionel says. "His are the best Projectionist paintings I have ever seen."

"I don't even know what a Projectionist is," Victoria says.

"Projectionist paintings are like holograms," Lionel says. "Imagine colored light projecting an image into the air through a crystallized canvas. The artwork in the air is the Projectionist painting."

"I bet they're beautiful," Victoria says.

"I already knew about Projectionists," Vincent says, sitting beside his corpse bride. "And I bet Gonzalo's paintings are beastly. Projectionist art defeats the purpose of painting."

"They aren't beastly," Victoria says.

"They are," Vincent says.

"They—"

"At any rate," Fiona says to Gonzalo, killing the couple's disagreement before it turns sour, "you must give us a tour of your childhood sanctuary."

"Yes, you must," Lionel agrees.

"What an opportunity," Henry, who sits on the opposite end of the table from Gonzalo, says, "to give us a glimpse into your childhood."

Yes, an opportunity, Gonzalo thinks. If only he could find a way to convince the Gunthers that he's no different than they. Maybe, if he treats them nicely, they'll take him back with them to society. "I could replace their son," Gonzalo says.

"What the devil are you talking about?" Fiona says.

"Well?" Lionel asks.

"I'm sorry. I got distracted. But my answer is no. I

20

will not take you to the dead side of the cemetery."
Gonzalo gulps the tea before lighting a cigar.
Between billows of smoke, he says, "How'd you even
get into that side of the cemetery, Lionel? Isn't it all
boarded up?"

"Well, yeah," Lionel says. He takes a drink before
he continues: "There was a hole in the plywood, and
a small rainbow was shining from the other side, so
I thought I'd explore, and once I stepped in, I
immediately noticed the collage of colored light. It's
magnificence in the flesh. And then in the color I
saw a top hat—a hue of blue brighter than the sky
and the corpse's smile, so warm and welcoming and
—"

"Enough," Gonzalo says. "Henry, have that
boarded up tomorrow."

Henry will comply with this command.

As Lionel drowns his discouragement with drink,
Gonzalo prepares a plan on how to win over Charles
and Ellen Gunther when they bury their boy. He
envisions himself in his cemetery, wearing all white
against the visitors' black, nostrils flared as he takes
in the sweet scent of fresh soil soon to be spoiled by
the stench of the coming coffin. As he stands there
in the center of the cemetery, halfway between the
wooden wall protecting him from his past and the
funeral parlor he has inherited, all the corpses rest
in their own coffins, waiting for the ceremony to
conclude, waiting to meet the new arrival.

Gonzalo hands his handkerchief to Mrs. Gunther,
patting her back with a calming, "Now, now."
Saying, "Blow." With care the coffin descends below
the land of the living. Gonzalo is glad Hank has
made it to his final destination undamaged, and he
follows this thought by giving Mrs. Gunther more
back-pats, saying, "Let it all out."

Invited guests begin to depart, disappearing
through the funeral parlor and into the place

beyond. One after another after another, and as each guest goes Gonzalo's gratitude for this moment grows. Before Gonzalo can rehearse his opening statement a few more times the last guest has gone.

"Take your time," Gonzalo says to the Gunthers, snaking a step closer.

The tears that drop from Ellen's eyes are constant and clear. And as they fall Gonzalo reminds himself to stay calm—he knows this will be his last chance with the outside world till the next burial which could be years away because the number of families with bloodlines binding them to this cemetery has become nearly extinct. But as the tears stop falling on account of Charles, who is wiping them from his wife's cheeks with his thumbs, the confidence is erased from Gonzalo's mind. The man pulls his wife's head close, whispers a kiss against her nose and holds it there. Soon the tears stop altogether. Gonzalo hopes this means they are already moving on.

"Mr. and Mrs. Gunther," he says.

"What do you want?" Charles asks.

An invitation, Gonzalo thinks, and says, "I couldn't help but notice the tears have stopped plummeting from your wife's pearly eyes."

Charles gently pulls his head back to examine his wife. "So they have," he says.

"And I see that you are ready to move on. But I have a proposition for you."

Charles is still looking into his wife's puffy eyes. Doesn't even acknowledge Gonzalo's gesture.

"I'm thinking," Gonzalo goes on, "that I could, well, replace your son. We could swap places, you know? He could stay here, and I could come with you. It'd be like he never left. You could even call me Hank if it helps."

"I like that, Hank," Charles says. "What do you say, Ellen?"

"Sounds nice, Charles."

"Ready to come home then, son?"

"I've been ready my entire life, dad." Gonzalo raises his arms and moves in for his first physical connection. But as he closes the distance his newfound father begins to wither. His face is sucked inward into nonexistence, and his mother's face resembles one much more familiar. Hank's gravesite starts shifting, too, and as the geographical change comes into focus Gonzalo discovers a near deserted table covered in sugar spots, crumpet crumbs and tea.

"You look so happy," Fiona says.

"I was," Gonzalo says. He downs the last layer of tea in his glass and wonders how long his mind wandered.

"Who were you talking to?"

"What do you mean?"

"You said 'dad.' Were you talking to him?"

"No."

"I don't believe you," Fiona teases. She reaches for Gonzalo's hand.

Gonzalo gets up and grabs Fiona by the blades on her back. "I would never talk to that asshole." His fingers bite into her bones a little harder as he accentuates each word. Under his pressure she whispers pain. Then, as sudden and surprising as a brain aneurysm, an uncontrollable urge usurps Gonzalo's dick.

He pushes Fiona to the floor and falls on top of her, kissing her teeth once he lands. From there Gonzalo's lips push south, pausing at each patch of decayed flesh until he reaches her cunt. Fiona's left labia has rotted away, but her right side still remotely reminds Gonzalo of the pictures his mother used to show him in sex ed. He teases Fiona's right lip with his tongue, and after a few moments, moves to the other side, forcing his way past the decay until he can taste her pelvis. Her bones quickly warm to his wet touch, and after a minute she moans. Soon the sensation causes her femurs to twitch and her spine to crack, and once that passes she pulls him up to her mouth. As the corpse uses her wrist to guide him inside, Gonzalo hears her bones crack in rapid succession, and with each pop he becomes harder.

BREAK

Years of laughter trails Gonzalo who, at the age of six, dashes through the cold cemetery air toward the wave of trees away from his home. Gonzalo has already passed the unoccupied field behind the funeral parlor and is now passing through the burial ground. As he reaches the last line of graves before the greenery Gonzalo notices that a peculiar change has overtaken the atmosphere. Unlike the coffins closer to home, which are full of corpses, these coffins appear to be empty, and an eerie sensation is churning inside Gonzalo's stomach, replacing the sadness that had stained his brain. Instead of breaking the barrier of trees and sprinting into the unknown, Gonzalo decides to play detective and investigate the case of the missing corpses. Pulling an invisible magnifying glass out of his back pocket Gonzalo becomes a hunchback as he waddles through the graveyard, desperate for clues. After searching for the tiniest hint of life for what feels like forever, Gonzalo gives up his search and sits against a tombstone to rest.

"What are you doing?" a corpse asks.

"Resting," Gonzalo says.

"Resting from what?"

"Searching for evidence of the dead." As Gonzalo says this he smells decay, and it dawns on him that he is talking to the very thing he is looking for.

"You're a corpse," Gonzalo says. "The perfect clue! Now I just need to find your coffin."

"You're sitting above it," the corpse says.

"I am?"

"Certainly," the corpse says. "If you don't believe me just check the name on the tombstone."

"Frank Arthur Oatsplash, 1800-1888," Gonzalo reads. And below it, "Here lies the ruins of Mr. Oatsplash, who died of a rash that erupted in his ass."

"That's not actually how I died," Mr. Oatsplash says.

"How did you die?" Gonzalo says.

"Old age," Mr. Oatsplash says. "Went to bed one night and never woke up. Died as peacefully as a peach plucked from its tree."

"Oh," Gonzalo says, disappointed. "I liked the other version better."

"It appears you weren't the only one," the corpse says. He gestured toward the tombstone.

Gonzalo starts to say something, perhaps to introduce himself, but before the words in his mind can coalesce into a coherent sentence, he remembers why he came this far into the cemetery in the first place and immediately begins to cry.

"What's wrong, child? Was it something I said?"

"Not you. Them." Gonzalo points toward the distant funeral parlor which is now barely bigger than a miniature mausoleum. And then to clarify: "My stupid sisters. They said the game isn't real. They called me a baby for believing in it, and then when I cried they called me a crybaby." A fresh round of water wets Gonzalo's cheeks.

"What did they say isn't real?"

Gonzalo takes a deep breath, trying to control himself. Eventually he says, "Baseball," while simultaneously losing all the control he had just

26

gathered and then some.

"That's nothing to cry over, child," Mr. Oatsplash says, comforting Gonzalo with contact.

"It's not?" Gonzalo says. He shakes off the hand on his shoulder.

"Of course not," Mr. Oatsplash says. "Baseball is obviously real."

"It is?"

"Why of course. Don't you watch it on television?"

"Yeah," Gonzalo says. "But my sisters said baseball is a show like all the other shows I watch and that the reason I keep on watching the same game is because we only have one episode recorded."

"And you believe them?"

Gonzalo nods his head.

"You can't believe everything your sisters say. Don't you know they'll say anything to hurt you?"

"Yeah," Gonzalo says.

"Then you can't believe them when they say things as absurd as denying the existence of baseball, okay? People even played baseball back when I was alive."

"Yeah, that makes sense, Mr. Oatsplash. I knew all along the game I was watching was real. Nothing else can explain baseball."

Before Mr. Oatsplash can respond, Gonzalo hears the tail end of the whistle.

"I'm sorry Mr. Oatsplash, but I have to go. See ya later, alligator."

"After a while, crocodile."

"Gonzalo, not crocodile," Gonzalo says.

"After a while, Gonzalo," Mr. Oatsplash says. He smiles. The old corpse watches the child dash back toward the funeral parlor, disappearing into the sea of tombstones.

Gonzalo stomps on the gravesite of Mr. Oatsplash, shouting, "Come out, come out wherever you are!" When Mr. Oatsplash doesn't appear right away, he pounds his feet even harder. Eventually he performs a body slam similar to the one used by his favorite superhero Corpse Man—half-corpse, half-man, full-fledged crime fighter. His body lands on the cemetery ground ass-first, dust collecting in the air around him. As it disperses Gonzalo catches a glimpse of the approaching Mr. Oatsplash.

Gonzalo wasn't able to sleep last night. After returning home from break, from his first meeting with his new friend, a crucial question swarmed him. For the first time in his life Gonzalo felt like a vessel for information to travel through. For the first time in his life, he felt like he was more than Gonzalo, son of the cemetery; he felt empowered. However, he also felt useless because he couldn't figure out how to formulate his question just yet. He knew it possessed a particular power to which he was unaccustomed to. As he wiggled through his school day, pretending to read his textbook—*Politics of the Postmortem: First Grade Edition*—he worked on how to word what his heart was speaking to his mind. After hours of thought class was replaced by break. As Gonzalo ran in the direction of Mr. Oatsplash, lighting his customary cigar mid-stride, he finally solved the mystery of the missing question.

Now, sitting beside the old corpse above his coffin, Gonzalo says, "Mr. Oatsplash, why are all the gravesites out here, except yours, empty?"

"Do you really want to know, brave boy?"

"Yes!"

"Okay," Mr. Oatsplash says, pulling the blue top hat off his head and resting it over his heart. "I will tell you, but it is a heavy story not fit for a child at all. But I also feel I owe you an explanation because you are a central character in its plot."

"That's crazy," Gonzalo says.

"If only it were, child. Now hush and let me get on with my tale." Mr. Oatsplash mimes zipping his lips together, meditating his present into the past, medicating his mind with melancholy.

"This story begins before you were born, Gonzalo. It starts with your twin sisters. On the girls' fourth birthday they ventured out deep into the cemetery. Deeper than they had ever been before. And as they stumbled across my resting place, as well as those of my comrades, they were amazed at what they saw. For you see, Gonzalo, this portion of the cemetery, the last few rows of graves separating your family's land from the forest beyond, used to be Corpse Heaven. We were far from your family and therefore were untainted by their selfishness. Each corpse gave everything for the other and in return received all every other corpse could give. We were one in everything we owned. And no corpse ever needed a thing."

"That sounds awesome," Gonzalo says.

"Yes, your sisters thought so, too." Sharing a thought with his sisters causes Gonzalo to gag, but Mr. Oatsplash doesn't seem to notice. "It wasn't long before your parents caught wind of your sisters' change in attitude. The twins told us the first time they thanked your father for making them food he threw it in their faces in disgust. Eventually your parents became so sick of your sisters' attitude that they beat the information out of them." Mr. Oatsplash pauses to see how his words have affected Gonzalo. Noticing that the boy appears to be unfazed, he goes on. "Your mother was also pregnant with you at the time. And fearing that one day, you too might succumb to kindness your parents stormed out to our side of the cemetery, keys in hand. They gathered all the corpses, one by one, and forced them into their coffins where they locked them inside for good."

"How did you escape?"

"I didn't. I had a feeling that one day something like this might happen. So I sculpted a key out of coffin wood and placed it in my tombstone while I waited inside. When your parents got to my resting place they assumed that someone had already locked me up long ago and moved right past me. Once they had finished I crept out of my coffin and watched them return home with smiles spread so far across their faces I wondered if they'd get stuck that way. Tell me, Gonzalo, are your parents' faces forever locked in hideous smiles?"

"No," Gonzalo says, laughing shyly.

"Oh, okay. Just had to check."

Gonzalo sits silently, brooding over what he has just heard. "So my parents killed all those corpses?"

"No, corpses cannot be killed. What your parents did is much worse. They trapped them in the small space of their coffins forever."

"How?"

"No one really knows the mechanics, Gonzalo. But as far as I can tell each tombstone is manufactured with a keyhole on top of it. And each lock has a key fit for it specifically. And when a corpse is inside the coffin, and the caretaker twists the key, something changes so that the corpse can no longer rise out of its resting place. Only the caretaker has the power to close a corpse's coffin, and once the key is turned it becomes part of the tombstone."

"Can't I set them free?"

"Never. Once a coffin is closed, it cannot be

undone."

"Mr. Oatsplash. I hate my stupid parents. Even more than before. I never want to be like them."

"I don't want you to be like them either," Mr. Oatsplash says. Then he whispers, "But I remember your father as a child, you're already so similar."

Gonzalo doesn't seem to catch the comparison. Instead he crouches close to Mr. Oatsplash, debating on whether or not he might be allowed to cuddle but discovers he doesn't have the courage to find out.

"I'll be right back," Mr. Oatsplash says. He dives beneath the soil, descending into his coffin. A couple minutes later he reappears in front of Gonzalo with something strange in his hand. "Here," Mr. Oatsplash says. "I want you to have this."

"What is it?" Gonzalo asks.

"Crystallized coffin wood," Mr. Oatsplash says. "It causes paintings to prism. And these are magic paint markers; they create colored light."

"Awesome," Gonzalo says, adding unnecessary emphasis to the last syllable. "Thanks, Mr. Oatsplash."

"Of course," the corpse says. "And with enough practice, one day you'll be able to create bodies of light that brighten up the entire cemetery by swirling shades of color together. Though I must warn you, you can never take these things to the funeral parlor. You have to leave everything here so I can store it in my coffin, otherwise your parents might see the light and come looking for me to lock me up forever. Understand?"

"Yeah, sure," Gonzalo says. He snatches his supplies from the old corpse.

"Let me show you how to use those," Mr. Oatsplash says, reaching for the present.

"Get away, these are mine!"

Mr. Oatsplash stays in his spot and shakes his head, looking toward the funeral parlor in the distance.

Over the next several years Gonzalo continues to visit Mr. Oatsplash every school day during break. With their time together they converse about the past—what it was like for Mr. Oatsplash before the coffins of his comrades were closed and what it has been like since. They also talk about Gonzalo's family—about his parents' vanity and the hatred he harbors toward them. Throughout these conversations Gonzalo promises Mr. Oatsplash things that fate will prevent him from keeping. He promises Mr. Oatsplash that he will never be a parent. Will never knock a woman up, dead or undead—whatever "knocking up" means. Will never be his father—despite the fact that Mr. Oatsplash notices more similarities between the boy and the man every day. And that he will one day leave this godforsaken cemetery and venture out into society to live a life similar to the one Mr. Oatsplash lived in Corpse Heaven. All these things Gonzalo promises, and all these things he will never keep no matter how hard he tries. But more than conversing, Gonzalo creates art. Using the pictures circulating inside his mind he creates a reality outside of his nightmare. Through his hand, and the seemingly never-ending supply closet of creative materials in Mr. Oatsplash's coffin, Gonzalo creates a paradise for him and his companion. During their days they live in their own personal agony, but for fifteen minutes they share a world that makes their lives worth living. In every collage of color Gonzalo tries to prism a picture of himself as a grown man with a cigar between his lips standing beside his only friend. Everyone else is gone; Frank Arthur Oatsplash and Gonzalo are the last two people, dead and alive, in the cemetery.

ANDREW J. STONE

LIAR

onzalo looks into the mirror and unknowingly sees the monster he vowed he would never become. He fails to see the hatred and greed and malevolence in his eyes. Past failures and present misfortune blinds him. He has pretended so long to be what he is not that he has forgotten who he is. Instead he sees a helpless broken man through blurred vision. Most of all Gonzalo sees his most recent failure: his inability to blend in with the Gunther family. He sees his last failed attempt at merging into society. "Goddamn Gunthers!" he shouts. "Don't they know they could have had their son restored?"

He hears Fiona's voice saying, "Gonzalo." Her voice saying, "I have something important to tell you."

Gonzalo looks past his pathetic reflection and glares at the girl behind him. Her face is devoid of flesh, her eyes hollow holes, black rocks resting in soft snow. A thin layer of skin wraps around her neck, and below it flesh is pasted over the bones in patches. Both breasts are flesh, though a worm has dug a home just below the left nipple. Fiona's arms and legs are bone, but her feet and hands are covered in strips of skin as if she were wearing worn down ankle-socks and gloves. As Gonzalo discovers the corpse's teeth have turned upwards, he sees

35

himself smacking the stupid grin off her face.

Gonzalo wishes he could be what he already is, wishes he could be his father. Instead he uses his weapon of choice: words. He reaches for his artillery and fires his voice, shooting, "What's so goddamn important, Fiona?"

The corpse doesn't bend beneath the bullet. The smile stands strong. "Okay," she says. She breathes deeply, trying to withhold her information as long as possible. Slowly, smiling, she says, "I'm pregnant."

"Impossible," Gonzalo says, followed by nervous laughter.

"I thought so, too," she says. "But after I felt the nausea, mind you the first wave of nausea I've felt since death, I became curious. So I took a test. Here." Fiona forces the stick into Gonzalo's hands. "The plus means positive. Positive as in positively pregnant."

"I know what the plus means," he says, trying to calculate what the pregnancy will imply. Then, "Where'd you find this? Were people fucking out in the cemetery again? Did it fall from some stupid slut's purse? How'd you get this damn thing?"

"It's mine," Fiona says. "I have a receipt."

Gonzalo gets up and moves toward her, saying, "Get out of here right goddamn now."

Fiona quickly backs out of the room, leaving the results in Gonzalo's hands before another word can betray either of their lips.

Alone, Gonzalo resumes his presence in front of the mirror. He looks at the + sign once more before throwing the stick into the shadows. Staring into strained eyes he now knows who he is—a liar. No longer blind he knows he hasn't kept a single promise to his only friend. Dear God, he thinks. And then aloud he wonders, "Mr. Oatsplash, what have I done?"

COUNTDOWN NINE

Two weeks have passed since Gonzalo learned his fate as a father-to-be. During the first week he took a vow of violence and silence against the corpses, responding to their inquiries with beat downs instead of words in an attempt to punish them for Fiona's fuckup. But after a day or two the plan backfired. Not only did the corpses immediately understand that conversing with Gonzalo would result in a brutal beating, and thus stopped talking to him, they also didn't seem to care whether or not they were graced with his company. As a result the corpses just figured Gonzalo had finally gone mad and went through their week without a worry while Gonzalo actually *was* beginning to go mad with internal anger and self-loathing until day seven when he erupted. Through his explosion, which was essentially just an episode of expletive epilepsy aimed at any corpse unfortunate enough to be vacating his vicinity, Gonzalo unearthed an epiphany. After expelling all his anger, he realized that just because fate wanted him to father a child didn't mean he had to be his father to a child. In fact having a child could end up being a blessing. Never before had he been able to break the barrier of society, but with a child he'd have another thing with him to offer the outside world. The more Gonzalo thought about the opportunity a baby would bring him, the more his mood lifted. As the second week came to pass he began to baby-safe the cemetery.

That is what he is doing right now: walking beside Henry, pointing out the potential problems a tombstone could present to a child, demanding that Henry disable the danger.

"Corner caps, Henry," Gonzalo says, gesturing frantically. "We need Styrofoam caps on the corners of every tombstone."

"Don't you think that's a bit excessive, Gonzalo?" Seeing the shift in Gonzalo's gaze, Henry adds, "I mean, when you were a boy none of the tombstones had corner caps and just look at you." Henry spreads his arms and smiles as if he is presenting the world with a man recently raised from the dead.

"Exactly, Henry. Look at me! I've been stuck in this goddamn cemetery my whole life. Sure, corner caps might not have made the difference I needed, but can I say that for certain? Of course I cannot! So maybe corner caps will make the difference. Maybe, once these are installed, they will prove to be our ticket out of here."

Sensing that Gonzalo is set in his stance, Henry concedes to the corner caps. "I'll have them installed by the end of the month."

"Excellent," Gonzalo says. He pats Henry's backbone before heading home happy with his day's accomplishments.

Despite Gonzalo's victory regarding the corner caps, as well as all the other cemetery chores he has already given Henry to do to make the place more baby-safe—eradicating all the spiders and snakes, cleaning the grounds of empty and broken bottles, erasing any evidence of his father from the funeral parlor—he still doesn't have the slightest clue as to how he should go about raising a child. Since Gonzalo secretly plans on closing all the corpses' coffins for the sake of his coming son, he won't have any help in fatherhood. Confidence he does not lack. He knows once he figures out what to do he will do it marvelously. It's just that at this point, he knows squat about bringing up a baby. But even his less than adequate infant knowledge cannot sour his spirits, because soon he will have the advantage of a baby to bring him into society. And seconds before Gonzalo completely loses himself in his social fantasy, a knock on his bedroom door brings him back to reality.

"Come in," Gonzalo says begrudgingly.

Hank Gunther walks through the door cheerfully, oblivious to Gonzalo's uninviting invitation, adoring his caretaker's decorations.

"What do you want?" Gonzalo says. He lights a cigar and blows smoke toward the intruder.

Gonzalo's cold, coughing voice brings Hank out of his reverie. Timidly he says, "I was wondering if you would have the time to give me that tour of the cemetery you promised upon my arrival."

"Goddamnit," Gonzalo mutters to himself. "What the hell, Hank? Now's just as good a time as any, right? Right?"

"Yes?"

"Goddamn right it is. Tour starts here. This is the master bedroom. See the coffin-shaped bed? See the dull gray drapes? See the plastic bats dangling from the ceiling? See them?"

Gonzalo continues presenting his room to Hank, who feels more frightened than fulfilled about finally getting to go on his tour. After conducting the corpse through the master bedroom, Gonzalo leads his newest guest away from his resting place and into the center of the funeral parlor.

EIGHT

Hank:

There are a few things to know about Hank. He loves the color red, loves to put things in his mouth and loves doing the opposite of whatever his parents instruct. These traits are nothing unnatural for a boy of eight years old; however, they are life-threatening if the parents of such a child own the largest plantation of castor plants in the country. This just so happened to be the case for Hank.

It is common for folks to start saying things like, "It's a miracle that the boy made it eight whole years before dying of plant poison." This is a valid claim to consider, but the reality is much less miraculous and much more materialistic. Owning the largest corporation of castor oil plants and plant products, it is only natural for Mr. and Mrs. Gunther to have hired security officers around the clock to keep their product safe. It is even more natural for Mr. and Mrs. Gunther to have instructed said security to, under no circumstances whatsoever, allow their son anywhere near the premises of the plants.

Mr. and Mrs. Gunther took an extra safety precaution by personally commanding their child to stay away from the plantation at all times or risk being grounded for the foreseeable future. It is in this extra step of caution where Charles and Ellen Gunther made their fatal flaw. Because if a boy's parents only spend five minutes a day with their son, and those five minutes are always another chance to warn their son against a particular action, said son will inexorably perform that action whenever the opportunity presents itself. Eight years, three months and four days after Hank Gunther's birth, the boy was presented with the opportunity.

After working the night shift as security at the Castor Oil Plant and Plant Products Plantation for three weeks Remington Jones came to the realization that the only way he could make it through another goddamn shift was to medicate his mind with his father's special moonshine. Despite the multiple warnings on the job application and on the premises to be alert at all times to keep the owners' son away from the products, Remi hadn't once caught the slightest wind of a child. He figured drinking on the job would be harmless, and if anything it would only make him *more* alert and interested in his work.

It didn't. After ten or twelve shots of the 'shine, Remi lay unconscious in a pile of puke. To make matters worse, what Remi did not know was that Hank had been watching him for weeks. Come three in the morning, three hours after Remi began his shift, Hank would sneak to the outskirts of the plantation and hide in the bushes as he watched the worker stand guard. Since discovering how easy it was to sneak out of the house at night, Hank had done this with every new employee, searching for a weak spot if one existed. For roughly a year Hank's efforts had proved worthless, but as he now stood in his hiding spot, watching Remi's unconscious form, he smiled with the knowledge that all his sleepless nights had finally paid off. On tiptoe Hank crept by

Remi's body and entered the Castor Oil Plant and Plant Products Plantation.

The excitement was so extreme that Hank almost hollered in ecstasy as he swallowed his first seed, compliments of the castor plant. But Hank couldn't stop at just one. Who knew when he would have another opportunity like this? He must make the most of his late night excursion. Hank started popping them into his mouth as if they were Raging Red Pop Rock candy. After a few minutes had passed he lost count of how many seeds he had conquered. He figured it had to be at least a hundred. And after at least a hundred more Hank didn't seem to feel so good. He assumed he had contracted some sort of stomach sickness because he ate so many of the seeds. Sick of the satisfaction of defying his parents, Hank started to head back to his room. But as he passed Remi, he suddenly had the urge to poop. And right there, on top of Remi's unconscious body, Hank had the worst case of diarrhea in the history of his world.

Mr. and Mrs. Gunther first found the drunken, shit-stained body of Remi, and Charles promptly fired him. As they followed the putrid trail into the trees they made another discovery. Charles and Ellen saw the cold corpse that used to be their boy.

One week later Mr. and Mrs. Gunther attended their only boy's burial. Charles Hank Gunther, 2006-2014. Tombstone reads: "With the passing of our beloved boy comes another passing—the passing of our beloved company, the Castor Oil Plants and Plant Products Plantation. May they both Rest in Peace."

As the clock chimes for the third time since midnight, Gonzalo creeps into his cemetery with a key in hand. He navigates through the tombstones effortlessly under the full moon, and after a few minutes he reaches the gravesite of his newest corpse. As he moves his hand over the marble tombstone's cool keyhole, he hears a slight snore escape the nose below him. Gonzalo unconsciously wonders what waking up will be like for Hank. He wonders how he himself would react to realizing that his eternity was to be spent suffocating inside a coffin surrounded by soil a few feet below the surface. Would he wake up trying to move through the wood like usual, and when he bumped into it, instead of through it, would he know his fate right then? Or would he bang against it? Once he realized his coffin was closed, would he bang anyways, fighting with the hope of the hopeless? But his thoughts vanish as he turns the key in the tombstone, and his curiosities are replaced by a satisfied smile as if he'd just hit a game-winning grand slam. In spite of all his wonderings, he now knows one thing is certain: unlike his own childhood, his coming child will never feel as if he/she must fight against other children—regardless of relation—for the love of a father.

From a few graves away, Gonzalo hears Fiona mumble something in her sleep. As he moves closer to her coffin he can discern the words of the woman from those of the bugs below and above him. She is saying, "Gonzalo, will you get me another Nightshade Salad? Hurry, please."

Earlier in the evening, the cravings had begun.

SEVEN

Gonzalo stands in front of an assembly of corpses, hands cupped around his mouth, mirroring a megaphone.

"Testing," he says to the fifty bodies before him, adjusting his hands to reach the right volume. "Testing one, two, three." One last tweak. That's better, he thinks. "Now, many of you might be wondering why I have called this mandatory meeting. It has come to my attention that some of you are worried about the tragic event of last month. But rest assured Hank is the only coffin that will be closed in this cemetery. You see, as a child I never felt like I was good enough for my father's love. I always compared myself to my sisters. After all they were twins, and two is better than one, right? Anyways, I cannot say for sure, but it is certainly possible that my insecurity regarding fatherly love just might have something to do with my many failed attempts to merge into society. So that is why Hank had to go. Without him my future child will not have to fight for my love and approval and acceptance as a father. And because none of you are children you have absolutely nothing to worry about. Again I apologize for the concern I undoubtedly caused some of you, but hopefully you can sleep easy now."

Gonzalo releases his hands from his lips and begins to walk back into the funeral parlor. He is about to leave the cemetery behind him when he hears many of the corpses agreeing with what they have heard, the loudest of which is Vincent. As a result of Vincent's agreement Victoria decides she disagrees with it and will in no way rest easy. She even says she detests the speech. The last thing Gonzalo hears before passing into the parlor is Victoria screaming, "Fuck that fucking good-for-nothing Gonzalo, and fuck you too, Vincent, for being reassured by his lousy speech." The last thing he sees is Victoria slapping Vincent across the cheek before running for the closure only their coffin can provide.

Six

Vincent and Victoria:

Victoria was the world's first professional deep-sea water ski champion. Vincent was her driver, personal trainer and longtime lover. They had been together for almost fifteen years and not once had they had a disagreement, not over a big thing like whether or not they should tie the knot, or even over a small thing like what their favorite color was. The answer to the latter was gray, the same color as their spirit animal, the great white shark. So it was only natural that on the day of their fifteen-year dating anniversary, they would both wakeup with a single idea molded into their minds: today is the day we wed. Not only did they both instantly know it was time to get married, they also knew they would have a deep-sea water ski wedding. Vincent was going to drive her through the deepest section of the ocean at a ridiculous speed causing a wake for the record books, and as the officiator pronounced them man and wife, Vincent would cut the engine as Victoria hit the artificial wave, catching some seriously gnarly air. As Victoria flew over Vincent's head mid-backflip, the groom would kiss his bride.

ANDREW J. STONE

The plan was put into action before Vincent or
Victoria even said a word to each other. From the
moment they woke up—not counting brushing their
teeth—Vincent had called an officiator, and Victoria
had called their camera crew. After that, Vincent
prepared his boat while Victoria called both sets of
parents, informing them of when their TV deep-sea
water-skiing elopement would air. Within an hour of
getting out of bed the schedule was set and Vincent
and Victoria were on their way to the water. There
was only one problem. Lost in their love, they forgot
to check the current migration pattern of the great
white shark.

Consequently, instead of cutting the engine when
the officiator pronounced the lovers man and wife,
Vincent   veered   left.   Moments   before   the
pronouncement he had noticed a school of great
white sharks swimming before them. Afraid of
slaughtering their spirit animal, Vincent played the
part of the sharks' savior and turned the other fin.
This resulted in him steering his boat straight into a
massive rock formation. Not only did this wreck the
ship, drowning Vincent with it, it also caused his
bride, sailing through the air without any control, to
splatter against the stone.

Vincent and Victoria died at the age of thirty-two.
To grant them the peace and harmony they shared
in life their friends, family and camera crew insisted
that they share a coffin. Their tombstone reads:
"May Vincent and Victoria find the same love in
death as they cherished in life."

They didn't.

After waking up in the cemetery Vincent and
Victoria realized that if they had disagreed with each
other just once the morning before their deaths,
they would have never died. And to compensate for
the fifteen years they spent in agreement, they
vowed to disagree with each other for the rest of

their deaths regardless of circumstance.

As the first glow of the sun infiltrates the cemetery Gonzalo stands atop Vincent and Victoria's coffin, waiting to greet them. But before he sees them, he hears their vicious voices attacking one another. It isn't until the sun shines high above the clouds that the corpses rise to the top of the soil where Gonzalo wishes them a good afternoon, and they proceed to debate just how good it is. The debate regarding the goodness of the afternoon never comes to a close. Instead it is eventually interrupted by Gonzalo as he confronts the corpses with a question. "Vincent, Victoria," he says, "I want to close your coffin. Is that okay with you?"

Victoria abruptly denies Gonzalo, and Vincent is forced to consent to the request. As he descends into the earth Gonzalo says, "My god Victoria, did you hear that?"

"Hear what?" she says.

"On his way down Vincent said you lacked the self-confidence to be locked in a closed coffin forever."

"He did?"

"I'm positive."

"Goddamn that son of a bitch. I'll show him," she says.

Before Gonzalo can say goodbye she has already closed the coffin on Vincent and herself. All he has to do is twist the key in the tombstone.

FIVE

From the patio of the funeral parlor Gonzalo addresses the corpses gathered in the cemetery.

"The accusations are true," he says into his megaphone hands. "Last month, I admit, I closed Vincent and Victoria's coffin." The audience is audibly startled, trying to disbelieve that their suspicions have just been confirmed. "But this is no means for alarm. The rest of you will surely be safe. To be honest, Vincent and Victoria gave me no choice in the matter. I mean, with their constant bickering, they resembled my parents when I was a child. And I just can't help but consider that maybe if I grew up in an environment that encouraged spouses to build each other up, as opposed to tear each other down, I wouldn't have had to fight my way into society, a fight that I have failed again and again. Ask yourselves, could a father who loves his child allow his child to be brought up in such a negative environment? That's the question I considered before closing Vincent and Victoria's coffin. If I hadn't done what I did I might as well have forced Fiona into an abortion because I would be aborting our chances of connecting with society. That is why I closed the couple's coffin and why I will not close yours. So be comforted, my corpses, for you have nothing to worry about. Be excited for our new arrival. My child will be here in five months."

FOUR

Lionel:

Lionel was a lifelong explorer. As a boy growing up in Brooklyn, he'd leave his house while his parent's were at work, take a bus to Manhattan and explore Central Park. One time he'd even forgotten to come home and camped out in the park for a week. As a man he'd often leave his family for months at a time via airplane in order to explore the African jungle. One time he'd even forgotten about his American family and, abroad for a year, started an Ethiopian family. As a grandfather he explored the attic in his son's house. He loved traveling through the jungle of time as he scavenged through photo albums recalling the trips he took with his son and the times when all his children were together. One time he'd even stayed in the attic so long that when he came down into the house half-asleep, he lost his footing on the stairs and fell to his death. He was eighty-four when he died. His burial reigns supreme in bringing the most people into Gonzalo's cemetery at one time. Guests came from every continent to see Lionel laid into the earth he loved so much. Guests came from every nation to see the tombstone that states: "Here lies Lionel, who was never at home in life, and with any luck will never be at home in death."

Gonzalo finds Lionel close to the boarded up section of the cemetery, trying to recreate the hole in the plywood that Henry had patched up. As Gonzalo moves closer to Lionel he sees a cluster of color escape through the tiniest bit of progress the explorer has made. Lionel is so entranced by the beauty before him that he doesn't hear Gonzalo's swift steps behind him. As Gonzalo greets Lionel he throws the corpse's head through the small hole he has recreated, simultaneously rendering the explorer unconscious and the blockade useless. Gonzalo then pulls Lionel back to the living side of the cemetery and a coliseum of color replaces the gaping gap where the explorer's head recently rested. Gonzalo drags the corpse by his hair through the grass to his gravesite. And when they reach their destination, Gonzalo kicks the corpse into his coffin and waits for him to wake.

Lionel slowly sits, grounded by grogginess. He sees Gonzalo through the grass above him and begins to ask what happened, but his memories supersede his words as he sees the sun shine against the bronze key. "Goddamn you, Gonzalo," Lionel says.

His caretaker closes the coffin.

THREE

"As you all know Lionel was a lifelong explorer. And while exploring on its own is not a bad thing, when it becomes the only rule to live by, all others are forgotten. And as a result, Lionel could not resist the temptation to break into the forbidden side of the cemetery. This disregard for order is unacceptable here. As a child the only thing my parents respected *was* a disregard for order. Although growing up in a world without order doesn't equate as to why I failed to merge into structured society, it certainly didn't assist the transition. Therefore Lionel had to go. But that doesn't mean any of you have to go, too. As long as you put my son first I promise you that you will enjoy your stay here, and that we will all get along swimmingly. And relax, the baby's birthday has almost arrived."

Two

There are complications. It is the third trimester, thirty-three weeks into pregnancy, and Fiona's bones have brittled.

Gonzalo goes to Fiona in the middle of the night and knocks on her tombstone softly. And after a couple minutes she slowly floats to the surface and is greeted by Gonzalo, who is extending a Nightshade salad. "For the mother of my child," he says, admiring her belly, a big bump of bone partially covered by small islands of skin. Fiona takes the plate from him and smiles, but before she can take a bite Gonzalo grabs her and lifts her into the air. "May I have this dance, dear?" he asks. The corpse complies.

Gonzalo leads Fiona in the dance of the dead, twirling her by the hips as she waves her arms above her head. The air breathes through Fiona's bones, and a soft susurrus sings through the silence. Together, if even just for a short segment of the dance, their bodies become one, life and death coalesced. Beauty this bright is destined to die. As Gonzalo twirls Fiona away from him, extending his hand to catch hers, preparing to pull the corpse close again, Fiona's right forearm detaches from her elbow. Gonzalo stands staring at the limb in his hand, contemplating the reality of the rupture, of the severed hand he now holds, of the sounds of a branch cracking. Fiona is falling, reaching out for Gonzalo's arm, her phantom limb incapable of connecting.

She crashes.

Her left elbow bangs against her hip as it simultaneously bats the ground, breaking both bones in the process. Fiona doesn't feel pain but immediately fears for the safety of her child. And then she fears for her own safety. She knows that delivering a dead baby is a death sentence.

As fear flexes its muscle Gonzalo approaches Fiona, who is lying in the fetal position, trying to keep her bone structure intact. He raises her severed hand as he comes within reach, but just before bashing it against her skull, scattering splinters of bone throughout the soil, he thinks of the damage that could do to his child. Instead Gonzalo says, "What the fuck is wrong with you? Are you trying to kill my kid?"

"No," Fiona says. "Our kid is killing me."

"Bullshit! You think I'm that fucking ignorant? Corpses can't die."

"I thought so, too," Fiona pleads. "But this thing inside me, it isn't completely corpse. And being wholly corpse myself, there are complications."

"What kind of complications?"

"Mainly, the complication of calcium. My body can't sustain the calcium I eat or drink for the child. So the thing inside me is literally eating and drinking it off my bones. My very skeleton is being consumed from the inside out. And there is nothing anyone can do to stop it from happening. I've become brittle."

Gonzalo prepares to show her how senseless she sounds. Everyone knows corpses cannot die. It is impossible. But then he realizes it's impossible for corpses to carry children inside them, too. Maybe one impossibility can create another. Instead of proving to Fiona that her bones aren't brittle, Gonzalo picks her up gently and cautiously carries her to her coffin. He lays her against the soil, and she slowly sinks to the coffin below. Under the stars he sings her his sorrows until she falls asleep.

ONE

Henry:

Henry had a secret. He'd been committing the crime for a few years now and had never been caught. He'd been afraid to share his past—and present—with people because they could have turned him over to the authorities. Henry knew he was the last hope each child had. If he weren't there to kidnap them, how would they ever know happiness?

Henry didn't call it kidnapping. If he were ever caught he'd call himself a voluntary babysitter. It's important to note that Henry never harmed the children he babysat but did exactly the opposite. Henry only watched children of abusive parents—sometimes emotional but mostly physical. Typically he'd spy on a family for months until he knew their routine better than they did. But this wasn't a typical babysitting situation.

Henry was walking toward the Rosewater residence as he had planned. Mr. Rosewater had been beating little Bobby for weeks. He would come home from the bar a little more than buzzed and, depending on how the Mets played, Bobby either got beat with a bat or a belt. The Mets lost more often than they won, so Bobby bled himself to sleep most nights after being beaten by his father's favorite bat.

Instead of turning right at the end of the block and walking the last half-mile to the Rosewaters, Henry kept walking straight. On the other side of the street he heard a little girl scream.

When Henry arrived at the house he peered through the windows and couldn't see the girl inside. In the bedroom he saw two people preparing to fuck, but there was no girl. As he walked toward the backyard, he started to hear near-silent sobs. Henry peeked over the brown fence and saw a girl no older than ten tied to a post on the patio by a leash connected to the dog collar around her neck. Both her wrists appeared to be broken so she wouldn't be able to set herself free. Without hesitation Henry hopped the fence and hurried to the little girl's side, trying to calm her along the way. "It's okay, child. I'll set you free and everything will be fine."

All she said was that she wanted her mother.

"And you shall see her soon. But right now let's get you off that leash."

"No I won't," the girl said as the sobs increased in volume. "Daddy said she'll be gone for a few days and that we were going to be staying with my other mommy, the one my real mom doesn't know about because if she did bad things would happen."

"Is this your other mommy's house?" Henry asked, unhooking the collar from the leash.

The girl nodded her head.

"Come on," Henry said. "Let's take you to the doctor so your arms won't hurt anymore. And afterwards I'll buy you anything you like."

The girl nodded her head again and followed Henry through the backyard and off the property.

Henry had an appointment for Bobby and himself at Candy World that day but decided on his walk to the hospital that he would have to call and see if he could reschedule. As the hospital came into view Henry realized he didn't even know the girl's name. "Sally," she said after he asked. That's how he introduced her to the receptionist at the hospital—as Sally, his daughter. A nurse led them into the doctor's office, and the doctor came in and asked how Sally broke her wrists. Henry told him that it was a merry-go-round accident, and the doctor set both of her arms without any more questions. Sally yelped each time he snapped the bone into place, but after they were put in pink and blue swirled casts, just like cotton candy she had said, she seemed to be in a better mood.

Outside of the hospital Henry asked her what she wanted.

"I want to go to the Design-A-Dog Factory," she said. "I've always wanted a dog!"

Henry wondered if she knew they just made stuffed animals there. He decided that even if she didn't know he would allow her to bask in her happiness for as long as possible, no matter how misguided, because he knew he wouldn't be able to bring himself to tell her the truth. "Then let's go get you the best dog ever," he said.

When they arrived at the Design-A-Dog Factory, Sally screeched.

"Is everything all right?" Henry asked.

"It's all so perfect," Sally said.

Sally designed a purple poodle. The dog wore green glasses that looked like a horizontal picket fence, a black cape with a purple SP embroidered on the back and green high-top sneakers.

On the walk back to Sally's other mother's house she told Henry that the SP stood for Super Poodle, that purple and green were her real mommy's favorite colors and that she had always wanted a pet poodle. Henry told her it was a beautiful dog as he bent over to pet the poodle's head peeking out of

Sally's arms, which were wrapped tightly around the base of its body.

When they got to the street where Henry would leave Sally he told her that everything would be okay, that he'd visit her again soon. She made him pinky promise, and as he did he told her that he wasn't crossing his fingers or toes. For the last time that day Sally smiled.

They reached the fence blocking the backyard, and Henry hopped over it so he could open the gate to let Sally in. They walked back to the porch, and Henry reattached the leash to the dog collar. Sally asked why she had to be tied again when it was obvious she had left. She reminded Henry that she had two new casts and a Design-A-Dog. Before Henry could answer, the back door swung open, and Sally's father stormed out with a shotgun.

"You fucking creep," he said. "Get the fuck away from my sweet little Sally."

"I was just—" The sound of the shotgun cut Henry's sentence short. As his brains blew into the grass, Sally screamed.

Gonzalo stands before Henry, dictating his every move as he makes the cemetery more baby-safe. "Now place that pole here," Gonzalo says. "Easy does it, easy, good!" Gonzalo is having Henry build a massive playpen on the patio of the funeral parlor. "Just one last pole," Gonzalo says, directing Henry where to install the last piece of the eight-piece puzzle.

Once Henry is finished Gonzalo offers him a fresh Long Island Iced Tea and walks him back to his coffin. As they reach his resting place Gonzalo says, "I need one last favor from you, Henry."

"Well, let's hear it."

"I need you to let me close your coffin."

"Why, Gonzalo? I did nothing wrong." Henry is genuinely confused about Gonzalo's request, and beneath the confusion lies hurt.

"Because, Henry, it is the only way. My child cannot be raised around corpses. It is unhealthy. All my life I lived with corpses and I have never been able to leave this cemetery successfully."

"I know that," Henry says. And then with hope, "Gonzalo, I can help your child. I used to help kids all the time when I was alive. I could teach the kid the ways of society. I can keep the cemetery baby-safe."

"I'm sorry, Henry, but you can't. Mr. Oatsplash believed he could do it, too, but it just will not work. There is only one way for you to save this child's life, and this is the last life you have a chance of saving."

"What can I do?" Henry says. "I'll do anything, Gonzalo. Anything to save a child."

"I need you to lie in your coffin so I can lock you inside."

Interlude

Frank Arthur Oatsplash:

At the age of fifty-seven Frank Arthur Oatsplash claimed to be the world's first dinomancer. Those who heard of his magic were skeptical at first, but after showing them the decayed dinosaur carcass, and after communicating with the dinosaur's departed spirit during a spontaneous séance, the skeptics quickly became part of Oatsplash's sect. This is what the dinosaur from beyond the grave said: follow the one who has raised Tyrannosaurs Rex, and he will bring you the blessings of the dinosaur.

Frank led his cult of fifty deep into the forest to live communally under the guidance of the Great Dead Dinosaur. Through his séances Frank learned the secrets to living a fulfilling life like those lived by the dinosaurs millions of years ago. And with this information he taught his followers the importance of sharing possessions and property, finances and flesh. In this manner they lived, and with the help of the Great Dead Dinosaur, they needed nothing.

Of course, the Great Dead Dinosaur was a hoax. Frank was an artist and created the Tyrannosaurs Rex replica over a period of years. He made his creation look decayed by covering the creature in weathered scales scalped from alligators' underbellies. The voices coming from the Tyrannosaurs Rex during séances were really just recordings coming from a phonautograph. The recordings on the phonautograph were in German which might as well have been the tongue of the dinosaurs to the constituents of the cult. Before the séance Frank Arthur Oatsplash would read passages from his German copy of *The Communist Manifesto* to the phonautograph, and then he would place the recording device inside the Great Dead Dinosaur so he could eventually translate the dinosaur deity's instructions to his followers.

Frank Arthur Oatsplash wasn't comfortable with calling himself a Communist. Not only did he disagree with parts of the revolution, he also knew that being open about his political preference would only make him a social outcast. So instead of converting his comrades to a new and radical political ideology that they would never agree with, he decided to take the easier approach and become the world's first dinomancer.

Under the guise of dinomancy Frank created the perfect commune. In the beginning none of his followers questioned the Great Dead Dinosaur because they simply felt blessed to be part of the chosen. Unfortunately for Frank the ease with which he deceived his comrades into joining his cult would later prove to be its demise.

Despite telling the six-year-old Gonzalo that he passed peacefully in his sleep, the truth isn't so peachy. Frank Arthur Oatsplash was eighty-eight and had been a dinomancer for thirty-one years when his cult uncovered the truth and hanged him.

A month before Frank was murdered one of the cult members became suspicious of the messages of the Great Dead Dinosaur. This member believed the lives the Great Dead Dinosaur was telling them to live were hauntingly similar to the dictatorial dream of the Socialist Labor Party of America. After sharing the party's platform with his comrades they felt the same way. It took a month for them to prove it, but eventually the cult found a copy of *The Communist Manifesto* in their leader's room while he was out working on a painting which would be displayed in their commune. After finding the book the comrades raided the carcass of the Great Dead Dinosaur and discovered the phonautograph inside.

Frank Arthur Oatsplash returned from his artistic retreat thrilled about his new creation. It was a painting of the Great Dead Dinosaur living in a commune and preaching to a colony of fellow dinosaurs, and Frank knew exactly where it would hang, too. Before he could place the painting in its new home his cult attacked him and destroyed the art.

"Now why'd you go and do that?" Frank asked.

"Don't feign ignorance, Oatsplash," one of the comrades said. He planted a punch in Frank's face. The fist floored Frank, and before he could get up bodies piled on top of him. Fists and feet made repeated contact with Frank's flesh, and at some point between the violence someone had slipped a noose around Frank's neck. Once the comrades got off their bloodied commander they dragged him by the rope to the nearest tree. There they tied the rope around a branch like a piñata, one end of it around Frank's neck and the other in the hands of the comrades. For the next few hours they played with Frank Arthur Oatsplash, lifting him off his feet just long enough for him to wonder if this would be when he would finally suffocate but never long enough to send him swirling into unconsciousness. To make the experience even more unpleasant the comrades would take turns experimenting with how many times they could smack the airborne Mr.

Oatsplash with a stick while they were dizzied and blindfolded. As it turned out the comrades excelled at beating their boss with a makeshift bat.

Frank Arthur Oatsplash didn't know what was going on when he finally fell unconscious and died. Besides the pain, which is where most his energy was focused, he had a vague notion that at some point it would all end, and he would be nothing. The longer time went on, the more he desired death. When it finally came, and he passed from this life to the afterlife, he was disappointed to discover that he still existed.

Frank found himself in a box. He didn't know where the box was, and he didn't know whether or not his treacherous comrades had put him in it. But when he came out of his coffin, pressing past the closed lid and the soil above as if they were water, Frank felt renewed and found himself in a cemetery surrounded by corpses. He accepted who he was and realized that if he accepted his political preference in his past life instead of becoming a dinomancer to cover it up, maybe he wouldn't have been brutally murdered.

With his newfound confidence, Frank Arthur Oatsplash approached a cluster of corpses in the cemetery and asked them if they'd like to join him in the creation of Corpse Heaven.

"It's too late to turn back now," Gonzalo says. He is seventeen, and there is blood on his body. Blood belonging to someone else.

"It's never too late, child," Mr. Oatsplash says. He is standing in his coffin, feet swallowed by soil as if he were on a ship sinking at sea.

"You're wrong. It has to be this way. There's no one left. This is my last chance." Teardrops bulldoze two identical paths through the blood, one on each cheek.

"Wrong again, child. The last chapter never has to stay true to its climax. Sometimes stories end with a twist." Mr. Oatsplash sinks deeper.

"But this one will not. I won't let there be a twist. This is my best bet, and I'm going to take it."

"It's not going to work. You're not yet ready," the corpse says, refusing to resist.

"Bullshit," Gonzalo says. "This is just how we planned it. And I'm going to make the most of it."

Before Gonzalo turns the key in the tombstone completely, he hears Mr. Oatsplash's last words. The decrepit corpse says, "Just like you planned, Gonzalo. Just like you planned."

Gonzalo completes the key's rotation, closing the coffin with a click, leaving behind everything Mr. Oatsplash had ever said or done, especially his last words. Feeling reborn Gonzalo struts through the deserted cemetery for what he believed would be the last time, smiling like the Cheshire Cat whenever he hears the knock of a corpse from the inside of a coffin.

ZERO

onzalo stares at the corpse as the first folds of flesh crawl through the crack. He takes hold of her skinless knees, spreading them further apart, commanding her to push. As the baby's forehead burrows itself into the light, passing itself into life, Gonzalo tells Fiona that he can see their child, that the corpse is doing great, that the head is almost out.

Then the head is out, popping past the decaying vulva like a hand from the grave popping past the last layer of earth. Next comes the neck and shoulders followed by arms flailing and legs flopping into Gonzalo's fleshy cradle. As he sees his child for the first time, Gonzalo screams.

Fiona asks Gonzalo if it is out, and he says it is, staring at the baby in his hands bundled in mold and breathing. The creature is actually breathing, and Gonzalo created it. Fiona delivered it and she asks whether or not the baby is a he or a she. Gonzalo, lifting a leaflet of mold, inhaling decay as he tries to discern the gender in darkness. He says, "It's a boy."

Fiona falls back against the grass, brittled bones breaking into as many pieces as there are hairs on the newborn's body. Gonzalo is unaware because he is too focused on gently wrapping a towel around his boy and wiping away the mold, using the mixture of their tears as a cleaning elixir. Once the tears are gone he brings the boy's forehead to his lips. He gives it a soft kiss and says, "Frank." He says, "Frank." He says, "Frank."

Despite the fact that the baby is nothing but bone from his shoulders to his wrists, from his thighs to his ankles, that he has Fiona's hollow eyes, that he is already crying and that he is half-corpse, Gonzalo loves his son. He says to him in near silence, "I will get you out of this place."

Then he sees Fiona, bits of bone deteriorating into dust. Gonzalo cradles his left arm, securing their son inside, and with his right hand he gathers the bone-bits and scoops them into his fist. He flees the site of the birth for the depths of the cemetery, feeling the bones in his hand wither away with every step. When he finally reaches Fiona's resting place, he throws her remains onto her grave, and below the light of the moon he sees specks of sand settle on top of the soil.

PART TWO
AFTER THE BIRTH

RECONSTRUCTING THE CEMETERY

After returning to the funeral parlor from the cemetery, Gonzalo fed Frank his first meal of formula milk. Since then he has been cradling his crying child and pacing around the funeral parlor, patting the newborn's back. Gonzalo cannot explain his inability to set his half-human son down, his inability to see the next step. Instead his mind wades through memories of Fiona, and he wonders what the corpse would do if she were still here. But Fiona reminds him of the coffins he closed and that makes him feel like his father. Refusing to accept the reality of the present Gonzalo pushes the past out of his mind. Finally something unseen switches inside Gonzalo, and he places the pacifier past Frank's lips, sets his six-hour-old son in his crib and in this silence he sees the solution.

Gonzalo strides through the open field behind the funeral parlor as the sun begins to arch into the day. He holds his hands around his eyes as if they were binoculars, avoiding the visuals of the closed coffins his feet now carry him past. He hears the dull thump of Lionel's body banging against the barrier of wood, hears Vincent and Victoria debating the day of the week without any success—being underground they have no sense of time, and although Vincent strongly senses it is Sunday Victoria is absolutely sure it is Tuesday. But they are both far from Friday. Gonzalo closes his eyes as he moves his hands to his ears, plugging both with a pointer finger, trying to kill the voices of the corpses he has damned. Despite his best efforts he still clearly hears Hank's sobs and Henry's babysitting monologue as he makes his way deeper into the cemetery. Without his vision Gonzalo walks into the wooden wall separating the closed coffins of his childhood from the closed coffins of the past nine months.

Having reached his destination, Gonzalo retrieves the axe from his belt, raises it above his head and releases all the power he possesses. The sound of the axe splintering the wall and the volume of voices from the coffins come together. As Gonzalo chops into the color on the other side the chants of corpses long suppressed join the cesspool of sound. The man hacks at the wall wildly, trying to erase the presence of the deceased. But as the swing of the axe increases, the underground voices grow louder and with them comes the incessant reminder of what Gonzalo has done.

Still, Gonzalo cannot acknowledge that he is worse than the creature he has spent his twenty-four years of existence trying to repress, trying to recreate and redeem. The image he entertains of himself is still the one of his father's victim, who is improving the world of the cemetery against the odds. With this scene set in his mind, he projects the caricature of his father onto the protests of the bodies locked below the earth; he projects the history of his own actions onto the corpses. The wall begins to splinter under the force of his axe, contaminating Gonzalo with clusters of color.

Once the wall has been destroyed Gonzalo gathers the wood so he can recycle it and resurrect the blockade, this time encompassing all the coffins in the cemetery. Over the next several months Gonzalo intersperses fathering his son with the reconstruction of the cemetery and sleep. He nurses the nonexistent relationship between him and Frank with the future. He tells himself that once the wall is up, barricading every gravesite in the cemetery, leaving a stretch of grass as big as a baseball field between the massive solidified fence and the funeral parlor, his relationship with his son will finally flourish. This insight fuels Gonzalo with cravings, and sooner than he anticipated, the new wall has been constructed, keeping the cemetery safe from the corpses closed in their coffins.

ANDREW J. STONE

THE MORTUARY MONSTER

"There's a monster within those walls," Gonzalo says to his son. They are sitting on the patio of the funeral parlor, and Gonzalo is pointing through the cigar smoke seeping out of his mouth toward the boarded up side of the cemetery beyond the long stretch of grass.

"What kind of monster, Daddy?" the corpse child says. Frank is five years old, and he scratches the insides of his hollow eyes.

"The worst kind," Gonzalo says, running his fingers through his thin black hair. "The Mortuary Monster."

Frank shakes bumps off his body and bones. "What's it look like, Daddy?"

"I've only seen it once, the day you were born, but I'll never forget that face," Gonzalo says, recalling the fabricated past. "At first the face was blank, flat. It had no lips or eyes or nose or bones. Just a mass of mess. But as it approached your mother, who rested against the ground after giving you your life, the face began to open up, and soon it was a ring of flesh wrapping around a doughnut hole throat, bending down to vacuum up your mother. And once the creature ate the corpse, his features were highlighted with Fiona. The color of decay covered

81

his nose, which now grew bone bumps. The eyes became moldy indentations, and the mouth turned pale-pink, scarred with serration. And more than that the head grew three times in size, stretching its features, until its chin reached as low as the monster's belly. And once it stopped growing, the gray hue of the cemetery masking its face lifted, and in its place shined a collage of rainbow color, making the grotesque features appear to be characterized by a cartoon—neon flesh scooped out in places and pasted to others."

Gonzalo pauses for air, and Frank succumbs to the fear his father is trying to instill. Gonzalo goes on, "If you ever see color seeping into the cemetery from the walls, you need to notify me immediately. Because where there is color the creature is close."

Frank nods, says nothing. Together Gonzalo and his son let their eyes drift through a layer of smoke toward the wall dividing the cemetery.

Birthday Cake

It's Frank's seventh birthday. Gonzalo is playing catch on the patio with his son when they hear a knock coming from the front of the funeral parlor. Gonzalo leaves the baseball with his boy as he walks through the main room toward the wooden door. The hinges creak as he opens it, and standing on the front step is the family's deliveryman. Despite his bald, liver-spotted head and sunken gray eyes Gonzalo still sees the black hair and baby blue irises he knew as a child.

"Took you long enough," Gonzalo hisses. "Did you remember the special order?"

"Yes, yes," the deliveryman says. "Everything's out in the car."

"Better be," Gonzalo says, handing over the money.

The deliveryman leads Gonzalo out to the hearse with *Hole Foods* spray-painted along the side and opens the trunk. In the back of the car rests an open casket full of plastic grocery bags.

"Where's the special order?" Gonzalo asks.

"Behind the casket," the deliveryman says. He goes to the side door, opens it, and reaches behind the coffin to retrieve the pink cardboard box.

"Let me see it," Gonzalo says. After the

deliveryman lifts the lid Gonzalo sees his son's birthday cake, the one he always dreamed of having as a child. He takes the cake from the deliveryman and brings it into the funeral parlor. After that he returns for the month's worth of groceries and once those are inside he slams the door on the outside world.

Back on the patio Gonzalo asks Frank to toss him the baseball. Once Gonzalo catches it he runs out to the grass, winds up his arm and throws it back as hard as he can. Frank fields the line drive with almost half the enthusiasm his father displayed while pitching it. As Gonzalo waits to get the ball again, he wonders why his son is lifting it into the air, inspecting it as if the stitching had come undone and the leather were peeling. Gonzalo doesn't understand why Frank lets the ball fall, thumping against the patio before rolling into the grass, or why the boy is sitting back down at the table. To compensate for his confusion Gonzalo sprints toward his son from the field. "Ready for your birthday cake?"

"Yeah, Dad," Frank says, smiling for the first time of the day.

"One birthday cake coming right up," Gonzalo says. "But don't forget to cover your eyes. You don't want to ruin the surprise."

"They're covered!" Frank says, resting his hands over the hollow holes on his face.

"And no peeking," Gonzalo says. As he walks by the boy, he rubs his hand through his son's black hair, admiring his youth and the opportunity he is giving him to join society.

Inside the funeral parlor Gonzalo lifts the cake out of its box and places it on a porcelain platter. He sticks seven black and white spiral striped candles in the cake and then carries it toward the patio. Before he walks out the back door, he says, "Are your eyes still covered?"

"Yes," Frank says, much louder than necessary.

"Good," Gonzalo says. Every few steps he slows down, waiting for Frank to ask if he can uncover his eyes. Each time Gonzalo swiftly says, "No peeking," before resuming his walk. After each exchange the excitement between father and son increases.

Finally Gonzalo sets the cake down in front of Frank, wishing him another happy birthday and telling him he can uncover his eyes. By now Gonzalo has more anticipation for the big reveal than his son does. This is one of the moments he had always wanted as a child—his father bringing him a baseball birthday cake for the two of them to share. Instead his father would give him a list on each of his birthdays containing the new chores that his extra year of life would enable him to complete. But none of that matters now because it is just him and his son and the birthday cake between them.

"A baseball cake?" Frank asks.

"Yes, son, a baseball cake! It's even round like a ball, too. See?" Gonzalo points out the obvious.

"Yeah, Dad, I see," Frank says, trying to eat his feelings.

"Well?" Gonzalo says, unable to detect the disappointment. "What do you think?"

"I don't like baseball, Dad," Frank says. "I don't even like playing catch. And I wanted a coffin cake with corpses on it."

Gonzalo is surprised to hear this from his son. Ever since his son's birth they loved baseball. It was their thing, the only thing they seemed to have in common these days. But despite the hurt Gonzalo decides to deflect the truth and ignore Frank's clearly miscommunicated cake desires and instead use this as a teaching moment. "Frank," he says, "that's no way to act when someone gives you a gift. When someone has given you something, you have to say 'Thank you, I love it,' understand?"

"But what if I don't love it?"

"That doesn't matter. You have to at least pretend to love it until the person who gave you the gift goes away."

"But what if they never leave?"

"Then you never stop pretending," Gonzalo says. He wonders if Fiona would agree with him on this life lesson if she were still here. After all she always told him to be thankful for things when she was with him. "Besides," Gonzalo continues, "it's your birthday, and we both know you love baseball. So be happy. You only get one birthday a year."

Frank nods his head in defeat. He tries to say "okay" but nothing comes. Instead he forces his lips to curl away from the ground. And eventually he does feel a little better. Good enough to ask his dad if he can eat a slice of cake at least.

"Not yet," Gonzalo says. "You have to blow out the candles and make a wish first."

"Okay," Frank says, trying to think of something to wish for. And then, "I wish fabric would grow in the graveyard."

"Damnit Frank," Gonzalo says. "You can't say your wish out loud because then it won't come true."

"Oh yeah," Frank says. "I forgot."

"Well do it again. And this time wish for something better. You only get one so don't waste it on something stupid like fabric in the field or last year's debacle of wishing the clouds would rain cloth." As Gonzalo says this he wonders how his son came to be so similar to Fiona.

"Okay, I'll wish for something else," Frank says. He covers his eyes with his hands, and his face shakes in thought. And then the wish washes over him, his best wish yet. Frank wishes he could talk to people outside the cemetery without the Mortuary Monster or baseball barging in on the conversation.

Frank wishes he lived with a friend far from his father so he could be himself. And then he uncovers his eyes and blows out the candles.

Once the candles are out Gonzalo slices the cake. As he cuts into the baseball he wonders what he did to deserve a son as strange as Frank. He knows that if he had half the upbringing from his father that Frank receives from him, then he would have had no problem leaving the cemetery as a child. Serving his son the first slice of cake, Gonzalo wishes Frank would understand how normal he has it.

ETIQUETTE

It's eight in the morning, and the table is set for dinner when Gonzalo, now nine, enters the kitchen. His mother welcomes him and says the time has come for his first day of etiquette class. Gonzalo just nods his head, hoping break will come sooner than usual. He tries to ignore his mother, who is now asking him if he were to ever come to dinner and find this table arrangement, what would be the first appropriate action?

"Pull out a chair and sit down?" Gonzalo says.

"Wrong!" A paddle cuts through the air and catches Gonzalo on the side of his head. "If you were to find this setup the first course of action would be to throw the spoons, knives, and forks onto the ground, quickly followed by the napkin and water glass. Keep the wine glass."

Gonzalo rubs the sting off his cheek. "Why do I have to throw everything on the floor?"

"Because, Gonzalo," his mother instructs, "eating with utensils is unnatural. It's something people do because they feel pressured into having good manners. Here we don't believe in belittling ourselves and our desires just to please others. So we replace good manners with good etiquette. Understand?"

Gonzalo nods his head as his mother takes a step back and presents her arms toward the table. The boy stops rubbing his cheek and steps forward. With an absence of ardor, Gonzalo tosses the utensils, the napkin and the water glass behind him.

"Very good," the teacher says, hitting her left hand with the paddle as if she were hitting her fist against her palm. "What's next?"

"Start eating?" Gonzalo says.

"Correct," the mother says. "But how do you eat?"

"With bare hands."

"And?" she says, drool drenching her chin as she anticipates the next strike of the paddle.

"And," Gonzalo says, trying to find an answer as he looks at the slice of coffin wood moving in his mother's hands. His face is still sore from the first slap, and he has to resist the urge to rub his cheek. He pictures the paddle making contact again, sees blood pouring out of his mouth onto his fingers. Blood on his fingers, and then his mind clicks. "And once I eat the meat I lick the blood and juice from my fingers."

"Wrong," she says, her paddle purpling the pupil's face. "After eating you chew with your mouth open, making clapping and suctioning sounds, like this." She pulls a pile of raw meat from the front pocket of her pants and shovels it into her mouth to demonstrate. "And once you have swallowed the food, then you lick your fingers clean of the juices and blood. Understand?"

"Got it," Gonzalo says, surprised that he is still unable to taste blood in his mouth.

"And the last lesson we will cover today is the most important of all," his mother continues. "It's time for me to teach you how to clear a table."

FRANK FINDS THE MORTUARY MONSTER

It has been almost a year since Frank has seen color coming through the wall. For as long as the boy can remember he has been doing weekly patrols around the wall's perimeter, checking for color clusters seeping through holes and reporting his findings to his father for repairs. Now at the age of eleven, far from the funeral parlor, Frank sees blue, green and pink rays shining from the other side. Unsure of how many years it will be before more color comes, and unable to kill his curiosity, Frank cautiously moves his hands through the rays. After confirming that his fleshy fists are unharmed he walks his hollow eyes to the peepholes.

On the other side of the wooden wall is a world of rainbows. Frank sees scattered among the shining shades all the tombstones his father has told him about, causing the beetles to bounce in his belly. It dawns on him that the graves are covered in color—that the creature must be close—and Frank jumps away from the plywood fence. He listens for the Mortuary Monster's footsteps, but they never come.

After five minutes of silence Frank creeps back to the blockade's decay.

This time Frank searches for signs of the Mortuary Monster. His gaze shifts from tombstone to tombstone, trying to find the source of the color. Once the boy feels confident that the creature isn't hiding behind any of the monuments he tries angling himself in a way so that he can see along the interior of the wall. Although he cannot see the twenty feet to his immediate left or right, Frank is able to observe the majority of the fence's skeleton and is satisfied with its lack of life. He steps back again, this time to look for a rock, but isn't able to find one. In need of some tool Frank sprints back to the funeral parlor, and after infiltrating his house undetected by his father, returns to the wall with a bat.

Frank lifts the bat in his hand and uses it to hammer through preexisting holes in the wood. Gradually it gives to Frank's force, and the boy creates a head-sized hole in the wall. The color becomes brighter than before, and Frank fears he has caught the Mortuary Monster's attention. Hesitatingly he sticks his head through the hole and absorbs the landscape before him. Nothing moves inside the blockade, and after a few minutes Frank is satisfied with the silence and continues to beat through the wood with the bat. And finally, after what feels like a year's worth of batting practice, the boy hammers a hole big enough for his body to pass through. Frank uses his shirt to wipe the sweat from his forehead and climbs into the color.

Frank surveys his surroundings for the Mortuary Monster one last time before he slowly makes his way away from the hole and into the sea of swirling color. As he steps deeper into the closed side of the cemetery Frank realizes that the hues hang above the ground like rainbow mist. The vibrant haze envelops Frank's body, and as he walks through it, it wades around him. Still, the fear has not left the boy's mind. He makes his way through his father's childhood sanctuary, focusing all his attention on the potential attack of the Mortuary Monster. Even hours later, as he slowly makes his way to the end of the cemetery, past the decorated tombstone of one Frank Arthur Oatsplash, the boy can only anticipate the possibility of facing a monster. Even though Frank has conquered countless acres on this side of the cemetery, he hasn't once questioned the source of the color, the authenticity of the creature.

It isn't until Frank returns to the hole he climbed through that he starts to suspect the reality of the past his father has presented. He knows that if the Mortuary Monster were as dangerous as his father claims, the creature would have attacked him by now. Frank begins to relax, and for the first time since coming into contact with the color he starts to see the bigger picture.

At first Frank catches pieces of the paintings out of the corner of his eye. He glimpses legs and arms, feet and hands. But whenever he focuses on an appendage it disappears back into the color. It takes a few minutes for Frank's eyes to find a fully developed appendage, but once he sees a distinct leg, the rest of the body begins to grow. Another leg appears, mirroring the first, and from there the thighs develop hips which sprout a stomach and chest. Two more appendages appear, phantom limbs materializing into arms of bone. And from the neck's nape a head emerges. On top of the head rests a top hat—a hue of blue brighter than the sky, and beneath the hollow holes Frank sees a warm smile spread over the corpse's lips. Beside the corpse, another being begins to surface, and once it has fully formed Frank realizes it is a caricature of his father. Somehow the image exaggerates the good in

Gonzalo to such an extent that if there weren't a cigar between the man's lips, Frank would have never seen the color as his creator. The painting looks more like a child's idealization of the man than the man himself. As Frank thinks this he finally understands that the color is coming from the artwork, not a Mortuary Monster.

Frank approaches the painting of his father and the corpse, causing the color to blur. He continues walking toward the image until it completely dematerializes into haphazard hues. As Frank walks beneath the mirage, he sees the crystallized coffin wood. He picks up his father's childhood canvas.

Holding the source of the color in his hands Frank scans the cemetery and realizes there are hundreds of images in the air, hundreds of sources. He drops the coffin wood canvas he is holding as he sees another painting. The color of this image again depicts a caricature of Gonzalo, again standing beside a corpse. This corpse though isn't a man sporting a top hat, but instead, a woman wearing a bright white wedding dress. Gonzalo is wearing a white tuxedo as he holds the hands of his bride-to-be. He is arching in for a kiss. Suddenly Frank realizes who this corpse is, and he sprints toward the color. And as the image dematerializes, the boy starts to read the names on the tombstones around him, searching for his corpse mother.

FRANK FINDS FIONA

Fiona:

As Fiona rose through the ranks in the fashion world, her dress designs put her work at the top of the red carpet wish list. Everyone wanted Fiona to design their dress, so it wasn't a surprise when the Voodoo Priestess rapper—Miss Mambo—demanded a dress from Fiona for her appearance at the music awards. What was a surprise was that despite the many warnings from her fashion friends Fiona took on Miss Mambo as a client. Fiona had been warned that those who designed dresses for Miss Mambo had a tendency to die in freak accidents shortly after working with the rapper. Fiona shrugged them off though, saying that all that Voodoo Priestess stuff was just an act to have a more interesting stage presence. Besides, she would say, even if Miss Mambo really were a Voodoo Priestess nothing would happen unless the dress was designed poorly, which was true. Fiona also claimed that she never designed dresses that were less than perfect, which was true, too. Lastly Fiona told her friends that when it came right down to it, she just couldn't pass up designing a dress that allowed for such artistic freedom and mystic aesthetic. The floor length dress Fiona would design for Miss Mambo would hug her skin in purple sheer, and an exact replica of the rapper's skeletal structure would be sown over the fabric. The dress would be worn with a python as a prop.

After Fiona finished the dress she believed it to be one of her best yet, and when she handed it off to Miss Mambo, the Voodoo Priestess agreed. Miss Mambo told Fiona that she loved the dress so much that she'd wear it for an entire week after the awards.

Unfortunately for Fiona, Miss Mambo lied. True, at the time she really did believe she'd wear it for an entire week. But a day after the awards aired, when the critics said the dress's intricacies caused vertigo, when they called Fiona's design a skeletal clothtastrophe, and when they said Miss Mambo herself looked like Skeletor's trashy stepsister, the Voodoo Priestess tore the dress off her body and torched it with her flamethrower, save for a strip of sheer, which she used to make a voodoo doll that she would place in her recreation of Fabric World when the time was right.

However, Fiona never listened to what the critics had to say because she believed it could only bring negativity into her life. At their best the critics could only say what she already knew to be true, that she designed the dress perfectly. At their worst they could make her doubt her ability to design. Fiona had already moved on from the Voodoo Priestess's dress and was now on her way to Fabric World to restock on white fabric so she could start her next project, which was to design a generically white wedding dress for a well-established actress.

Because Fiona was completely oblivious to the controversy her purple sheer skeletal dress had caused, she didn't anticipate what would soon be known as the Fabric World Freak Accident. Fiona entered the sliding glass doors like she always did:

subconsciously smiling and whistling whatever song was stuck in her head. She loved walking past the rolls of fabric that lined each aisle, lingering as long as possible as she inched toward her destination, inhaling all the fresh fabric scent her nostrils could handle. Lost in her love Fiona failed to realize that once she passed a roll of fabric, it started to unwind. When she reached the white lace in the center of the store, strands of sentient fabric surrounded her on all sides. And as she prepared to cut herself the first strip of white lace, the fabric attacked. The sentient strands wrapped themselves around Fiona's body as if they were flames hugging a corpse in a crematory. But before they could suffocate her Fiona's heart burst, causing blood to slowly seep out of her body and into each roll of fabric until everything she loved was a dark red.

Miles away Miss Mambo vacated her bedroom. She was hungry and wanted a sandwich. Alone on her desk in the dark a voodoo doll rested, mummified in fabric with a nail thrust through its heart.

Frank stands before Fiona, reading the epitaph engraved on his mother's tombstone repeatedly. It says, "Here lies Fiona: Fashion Designer for all who, in a freak fabric accident, did fall." And below her inscription Frank eventually sees another note scratched into the stone which reads, "This wasn't part of my plan, Fiona. You weren't supposed to die, too. We were going to raise our son together, just me and you."

Frank bites his lips, stifling a scream. In the

silence he digests the information, causing his body to quake. The tension continues to build in his bones until movement becomes the only method for release. Slowly he steps up to the tombstone, only stopping when he is within arms-length. Frank has never punched anything before. Although he believes he contains enough anger to beat his fist through a brick, the reality is that his punch can hardly break a twig. The way Frank winds back his right arm is far from natural, and when it hits the words his father wrote the day his corpse mother disintegrated into bone dust he winces. Frank pulls his arm back and, ignoring the pain, sends it into the stone once more. In his mind he will beat his father's engraving out of existence, as if he were an embalmer beating rigor mortis out of a body. But as Frank's fists connect with the tombstone the sleeves of skin covering his fingers begin to bruise and peel, and beads of blood desert his knuckles and dig into his father's inscription. Eventually the punches pound the blood into the tombstone, sealing the words his father scratched for his mother the day Frank was born.

Exhausted by the exertion Frank rests his raw fists at his sides and takes in the damage he has done. Specs of red are splattered all over his mother's monument, but most of the colored mess is concentrated near the bottom of the tombstone, making his father's words indistinguishable beneath the blood. Once his father is erased from his eyes Frank revisits the epitaph, forgetting about his fists, which now look more like bullet-bitten meat puppets instead of human hands.

Frank rereads the words engraved on his mother's tombstone again and again until he is finally able to break the disbelief. Understanding begins to settle in Frank's brain as he realizes that being half-corpse isn't the only trait he has inherited from his mother.

He now knows that his love of fabric doesn't mean anything is wrong with him like his father has suggested throughout his life, but instead it just cements the fact that he is his mother's child. With this realization on the forefront of his mind, Frank promises his dead mother that he will become a fashion designer so he can bring them closer together. Once he makes his promise he wraps his bones around his mother's tombstone, hugging it as hard as he can. Even though he doesn't say it, he thinks about how much he loves his mother.

EXAMINATION

Gonzalo is nine and waiting for his family to join him at the kitchen table. His etiquette examination will begin soon, but instead of studying his past lessons he sees himself far from the funeral parlor, on the edge of Mr. Oatsplash's coffin, as the old corpse shares stories of his communal living both inside and out of the cemetery. Between Mr. Oatsplash's stories, his favorite 'Fifties television shows and baseball Gonzalo believes he has a solid idea of what life is like beyond the graveyard. He fantasizes about when he will finally be able to leave home and what he will do. First he'll go see a baseball game. After that he'll find a family that loves him and will play catch with him. But his daydreams die as his mother serves dinner, and the rest of his family joins him at the table.

"Mother," Gonzalo says. "Would you mind passing me the bread and butter?" His father groans as Gonzalo says this, and if the boy were to look at the man he'd see that he is already preparing himself for a poor grade.

Gonzalo's mother doesn't say anything, but she lifts an eyebrow as she passes him what he asked for, letting him know he better be more cautious

101

with his manners if he plans on passing. Gonzalo restrains himself from thanking her and quietly spreads the butter on his single slice of untoasted bread.

"So, Mildred, Miranda, what'd you learn in school today?" Gonzalo's father asks.

They begin to say, "Mother taught us—" But Gonzalo stops listening. Instead he is back in the cemetery creating art while conversing with Mr. Oatsplash. "Teach me how to make friends," Gonzalo demands. He works on the drawing of his dream school, which he plans on filling with future friends. "So that the next time I runaway I will be able to sleepover at their house."

"You know, Gonzalo, that wasn't the only reason you were unable to stay away from the cemetery."

Gonzalo takes a deep breath. "If that wasn't the reason, then why couldn't I stay away? Because what I remember is the police picking me up at the park in the middle of the night and escorting me home."

"You were brought back here because you weren't ready to leave."

Gonzalo knew Mr. Oatsplash was going to say this. Every time he brings up leaving the cemetery he is reminded that he isn't ready. Still, he doesn't believe it. He knows that if he could make a friend or two, then he'd be fine. But none of the kids in society like him. They call him creepy. They tell him they hate him for being so strange and mean, but Gonzalo isn't mean to them. He's way nicer to them than he is to his family. When he ran away he brought them his father's prized possession—his great-grandfather's shrunken head. He risked the beating of his life for them, and they just called him a freak. Even then Gonzalo thought the exploration was worth the whipping.

"Why aren't I ready?" Gonzalo asks. "I've been preparing my whole life. I can't be here any longer."

"All I can say is that when you're ready, you will know."

"How?" Gonzalo says, trying to make Mr. Oatsplash see how important this is with his facial expressions.

"You will know because you'll no longer belong here." Mr. Oatsplash leans forward to see the picture Gonzalo has been working on the last few days. "It's a beautiful light," he lies. "The blue walls and the yellow roof are so distinct up close, but when I take a step back the color glows green."

"Thanks," Gonzalo says. After a minute he asks, "What light describes people?"

"I don't think it matters," Mr. Oatsplash says. "Just do what you usually do, use whatever color feels right."

"This needs to be realistic," Gonzalo says. "I need to see real people in the picture so I can practice talking to my future friends."

Mr. Oatsplash studies the single color coming off the coffin wood canvas and starts to understand how serious Gonzalo is about having friends far from the cemetery. Gonzalo has never drawn anything realistic before because when viewed from a distance the beauty of Realism becomes lost in Projectionism. Usually Gonzalo's art is abstract, a cluster of color that when seen from a foot away appears to be nothing more than bright rainbow vomit, but when seen from afar the light spreads into the world creating intricate images. Mr. Oatsplash steps closer to the canvas, and as the green disperses into a detailed school he says, "Still interested in how to make friends, Gonzalo?"

"Yes!" the boy says. He knows that once he learns how to make friends, he will be ready to leave the cemetery forever.

"It's easy," Mr. Oatsplash says. "All you have to do is be polite."

Before Gonzalo can respond his father's voice brings him back to the dinner table. He is saying, "Gonzalo, are you ready for your examination?"

Gonzalo shakes the memories of Mr. Oatsplash out of his mind and absently nods.

"Very good," the man says, smiling at his wife. "Begin."

"The first—"

"Goddamnit Gonzalo, this isn't an oral exam," the father says. "Show us." Mildred and Miranda laugh loudly at their brother, who creates hypothetical scenarios in his mind where his sisters are screaming.

Gonzalo begins to apologize but disguises it with a cough. He then prepares to show off his etiquette for his family. Gonzalo drops his silverware and picks up the massive mound of raw meat. He begins to inspect it for worms but his father bangs a fist against the table so Gonzalo quickly tears into it with his teeth. As he chews he obnoxiously claps his lips together, concealing the meat inside, and spreads them with a suctioning sound. His family sees flashes of steak as if his lips are a strobe light.

"Good," his father says. "What comes next?"

Gonzalo sucks the meat juice and blood off his fingers and wipes the remaining drops all over his shirt and shorts. After that he pushes his fingers into the stick of butter, separating a thick slice. He uses the heat of his hands to help him mold the butter into a ball that he throws at one of his sisters, so she can spread it on her piece of untoasted bread.

"Lousy aim, butterhands," Mildred says. She spreads her slice of bread through clumps of butter stuck in Miranda's hair. "Maybe you should get some glasses."

"Glasses don't help retardation," Miranda says, wincing each time a hair clings to the butter instead of her scalp.

Gonzalo tries to come up with a rebuttal, but nothing sufficient surfaces and his father shakes his head. The man says, "Surely your mother must've taught you more etiquette than just that. Did she teach you how to clear a table?"

Gonzalo nods but doesn't say anything.

"Well? Won't you give it a go? It's your only shot at passing." Everyone at the table looks toward Gonzalo in anticipation. They wonder if the boy will be able to do what it takes to clear them from the table.

Gonzalo stands on his chair and closes his eyes. His stomach muscles tighten as he lowers his pants and he moves his hands to the cheeks below his back, pulling them apart. He tells himself he can do this, and he pushes with all his power. Not even the slightest skid of gas seeps into the atmosphere. Gonzalo opens his eyes and sees the excitement on the faces of his family members. His father moves his hands forward, signaling that he can do this, that they all want him to pass, that he just needs to push. Gonzalo shuts his eyes again and pushes even harder. The insides of his eyelids transform to images of his anus expanding. Then the images begin to contract, and Gonzalo's etiquette plunges under the pressure. "I can't do it," Gonzalo says. He sits back down in his chair and retrieves the silverware. "I can't clear the table, and I can't continue eating without utensils. I'm sorry."

"What did you say?" The man springs to his feet, causing the chair to crash against the floor in the process.

"I said I'm sorry," Gonzalo says, trying to crawl into the depths of his chair.

"You know how much I hate apologies," the man says. He starts to walk toward his son with raw meat raised in his hand.

"I know, I'm sorry," Gonzalo says. "I mean, please

don't hurt me. I mean—"

The mound of meat smashes against Gonzalo's head, sending him and his chair to the wood floor.

"Next time, you will clear the table when you are told," the father says. "This time, though, you get a fat fucking F." He bends down over his son, pressing his knees against his chest.

"I'm sorry," Gonzalo says unintentionally.

The father's knees dig deeper into his chest cavity, and breathing becomes nearly impossible. "And where the hell did you learn such manners?"

Gonzalo starts to say Mr. Oatsplash but catches himself before the words leave his lips. Instead he says, "From the old television in the game room. From Lucy."

"I knew it!" The man uses his son's chest as a platform to propel himself back into a standing position. He says to his wife, "I told you, Emily, television is nothing but garbage. It teaches kids all kinds of misbehavior." And then to his son, "Gonzalo, you're the son of the cemetery, you should be outside commanding corpses, forcing the ones you like to play with you and the ones you can't stand to slave for you. Not inside watching a stupid box full of inadequate etiquette."

"But I don't want to be the son of the cemetery, Dad," Gonzalo says, unable to restrain himself. "I want to be more than just another caretaker of corpses. Some day," he continues, "I want to make friends away from this place. I want to play baseball."

"For fuck's sake, son," the man says, kicking the boy as if his foot were a bat and Gonzalo's face a ball pitched below the strike zone. "Can't you see the gift your mother and I have given you? Can't you see that you cannot be anything more away from the cemetery, only less? Being the son of the cemetery is the dream everyone outside aspires to achieve. Here

106

we can enjoy life without having to conform to societal norms. And once those in society die, they become nothing more than posthumous slaves from which we profit."

The father lights his cigar and takes a hit before handing it off to his wife. He exhales and smoke masks his son's face. The man continues, "So for your own good, Gonzalo, until you understand the magnitude of the opportunity we have presented to you and you master your role as the son of the cemetery, I must ban you from watching television or entering the game room. And if I so much as hear the slightest sound coming from that room I'll whip you with a strip of coffin wood forty times minus one. Understand?"

Gonzalo silently nods his head, tying to swallow the blood that has pooled in his mouth.

Then, to make sure his son understands, the man climbs onto the table and pulls down his pants. He slowly squats, and once he is in position, liquid shit slides out of his ass. He crabwalks on the table until shit has stained each plate and doesn't stop until he is hovering over his son's dinner. Once the seepage ceases, he gets off the table and grabs Gonzalo's plate, dumping the food onto the boy before breaking the porcelain over his head. As the crap coagulates with the boy's blood the man says, "Now that's how you clear a motherfucking table, understand?"

Gonzalo says he understands.

FUNERAL PARLOR FASHION

Frank is fourteen and sitting against his mother's tombstone, sewing the last sleeve onto his father's baseball uniform. He has been working on the uniform, as well as his own, since he first discovered his workshop on the closed side of the cemetery. After realizing that the Mortuary Monster was nothing more than a myth made by his father, and consequently discovering his mother's occupation, he convinced Gonzalo to buy him fabric, promising the man that he'd make them the best baseball uniforms ever. After all, he'd say, maybe the reason he could never get into the game was because he didn't have the proper attire. The idea relieved Gonzalo, and he bought his boy some fabric so Frank would be able to make the perfect uniforms.

Frank spent some of his time working on the uniforms like he promised, but most of the fabric his father purchased went to creating corpse clothes. Ever since the day he walked into the light and learned of Fiona's passion he knew that the only way he could grow closer to his mother was to embody her bones through fashion. For the last three years Frank has been secretly corpse-dressing, trying to meld his mind with his mother through designer meditation while more or less working on two baseball uniforms. That's what he is doing now as he sews the last sleeve: sitting against his mother's resting place, wearing his favorite articles of corpse clothing and creating scenes in his mind that his mother might have experienced after life.

He sees his corpse mother sewing a bone-white ribcage around a straight spine onto black fabric which she is making for a corpse suffering from scoliosis. Then he sees his mother sitting at the head of a table, hearing bone complaints from fellow corpses before assuring them that she has just the cure. She's back in her studio which, like Frank's, surrounds her tombstone, creating corpse clothes to cover the abnormalities of the dead.

Of course somewhere in Frank's subconscious he holds the knowledge that his mother was human when she was a fashion designer. Even her tombstone suggests that. Frank is also aware that having his father for a caretaker doesn't allow for the most enjoyable life. He knows this from his own experience, and he has the advantage of being his father's son as well as only being half-corpse. Frank can't imagine what his life would be like if he were fully corpse and unrelated to his caretaker. Somewhere inside Frank knows his corpse mother would have never been able to find the freedom needed for fashion in the cemetery, and that her inspiration came from life. But the boy cannot admit that to himself because that would destroy the freedom he finds in his mother. Frank needs Fiona to be his corpse mother or her identity is blurred with his father's, and then he would be corpse-dressing for nothing.

Frank finishes the sleeve and holds the jersey at arm's length, inspecting every inch. He knows that his father will love the graphic. Gonzalo made him draw a series of sketches so the print would be perfect. There aren't any words on the white jersey, but in the center is the outline of a big black baseball with white stitching. Inside the ball is a white illustration of the funeral parlor. But what Frank is looking for is mistakes in the design work. He slowly rolls his eyes from one seam to the next, making sure that every thread appears to be in its place. After half an hour he's happy enough with his work to present it to his father.

Instead of doing this right after he finishes it, Frank decides to use the rest of the fabric first. He's almost done with a new pair of corpse pants, this pair in the style of a corpse who is big-boned. Frank has small bones himself but has always wondered what it would feel like to be big, and once he sews the rest of the fabric onto his new pair of corpse pants, his curiosities will be quenched. As the bones become bigger Frank's confidence increases. Despite the multiple threats Gonzalo has made about never buying Frank fabric again, by the time the fabric is gone the boy is sure that his father will buy him more materials once he is presented with the new baseball uniform. After all the presentation will prove Frank's progress as well as his ability to design the perfect jersey, and without more fabric he will never be able to sew the last sleeve onto his own uniform.

Gonzalo has had it with Frank's pace. Admittedly he is no fashion expert and has no idea how long these things take, but fucking shit, surely his son should be done with two baseball uniforms after three years of daily sewing and several over-the-phone orders from Fabric World. As he walks through the funeral parlor Gonzalo has to resist the urge to break down the door of his son's room, and instead he tries to turn the knob. As he expected the door is locked which means that Frank is still sitting at his station sewing away. Gonzalo reminds himself that Frank said he'd be finished with his uniform this week and will finish his own in the next week or two, so he lights a cigar in an attempt to relax, inhales deeply and walks away from his son's room for the cemetery.

The first time Gonzalo became fed up with Frank's pace was almost a year after the boy began working on the baseball uniforms. Gonzalo was preparing to light a cigar as he walked toward the cemetery, but before he could strike the match he walked past the hallway leading to Frank's room. Seeing that his son's door was shut Gonzalo thought the boy was watching television instead of sewing the uniforms like he promised, and consequently rage rushed the man. Gonzalo banged his body against the door, breaking the frame in the process. As he barged into the room, cursing his son for his lack of results, he realized that Frank was finishing up the first pair of baseball pants. Once Gonzalo understood that his son had been keeping his promise, and that he really didn't have a clue as to how long it took to finish things in the fashion world, he looked back at the broken frame, pressed it into place and told his son he'd fix it in the morning.

Later that night, after finishing the baseball pants, Frank told Gonzalo that when he came into his room, or even when he simply knocked, it mentally took him away from his work, and at times it could take hours for him to resume. He used what happened earlier that day as an example and explained to his dad that whenever the door was locked it meant that the uniforms were coming closer to completion, and that if Gonzalo needed him he should try twisting the knob. If the door opened he was available, but if it stayed shut he was sewing and needed solitude.

Since that day Gonzalo hasn't so much as knocked on his son's door when it was locked. He didn't want Frank to think that he didn't trust him. Gonzalo's parents never trusted him as a child, and just maybe this misplacement of trust kept him from joining society. So no matter how angry he got at his son's apparent lack of progress he never interrupted Frank's work. Instead he savored his anger for dinner. In the meantime Gonzalo would stroll through the cemetery while he smoked a cigar, waiting for Frank to come out of his bedroom.

Just like on every other cemetery stroll Gonzalo has taken over the past three years the man dreams of playing baseball with Frank. He sees himself and his boy out on the field, Frank standing beside home plate with a bat in hand, Gonzalo on the mound with his glove covering his mouth, shaking and nodding his head to communicate with the imaginary catcher. Eventually he winds up his arm and releases the ball. His son swings the bat and beats the ball out of the park, hitting a walk-off homerun. Instead of getting angry Gonzalo tosses his glove aside and celebrates with his son as if they were teammates and had just won the World Series.

Halfway through this stroll, though, Gonzalo's daydream is interrupted when he sees color coming from the closed side of the cemetery. He heads toward it to investigate, and when he arrives he notices that there aren't any holes for the color to pass through. Instead a piece of wood shaped like a boulder has been dislodged from the wall, and he figures Frank must have something to do with this. The suspicion grows as Gonzalo wheels away the chunk of wood and enters through the secret passage.

Gonzalo finds Frank in front of Fiona's grave wearing pants with bones much bigger than his own and a skeletal vest so his chest matches his arms. On his head is a mask concealing his flesh with a skull, and there are two holes carved out of the fabric for his hollow eyes. Before the boy is a pocket-sized mirror sitting on top of Fiona's tombstone, and by doing different stretches and continually turning in circles he eventually sees every part of his body in the corpse clothes.

"So this is why it's taking you so goddamn long," Gonzalo says.

The boy jumps when he hears the voice, turning in the air to face his father and accidentally knocking the mirror to the ground. Frank tries to say something, but he can't raise his voice above a whisper.

"What?" Gonzalo goes on. "You think I wouldn't figure it out? That I wouldn't find you out here when you said you'd be in your room?"

"I don't know," Frank says.

"You don't fucking know?"

"I guess," Frank goes on, "I just never cared if you caught me. Because the worst you could do to me is kill me, like my mother, and if you did that it'd just make me more like her."

"I didn't kill your mother," Gonzalo says, creeping toward his son. "It was . . ." He glances at her tombstone. "An accident."

"An accident!"

"Yeah, an accident," Gonzalo says, inching closer to the half-corpse. "Everything I've done was to protect you. That includes what happened to your mother. And if you had just listened to me you'd have made it into society easy. But look at what you've done, who you've become. Frank." Gonzalo gestures toward the boy with his hands. "You're dressed like the son of the cemetery!"

Before the boy can respond the man tackles him. Gonzalo rips the fabric off Frank's body, and once it is all off he uses the strips to slap his son across the face.

A few lashes later Gonzalo gets off Frank to collect the rest of the fabric. Once it is bundled in his arms he says, "I'm throwing this fabric in the furnace. If there is more of this shit lying around this is your chance to tell me. After it's gone I never want to see this stuff in the cemetery again. Understand?" Frank doesn't say or do anything and Gonzalo retreats to the funeral parlor.

As Gonzalo makes his way out of the color and into the living side of the cemetery he questions if his son ever meant what he said about making baseball uniforms. He doubts Frank even thought about the jerseys after making the sketches, and the thought causes Gonzalo to walk a little faster. The man tries to fathom how his son could not only break his promise but could also use shipment after shipment of fabric to pervert his body with corpse clothes. By the time he reaches the patio of the funeral parlor Gonzalo is practically sprinting. After he tosses the fabric into the furnace he lights another cigar, takes a few hits and then presses the foot into the fabric until the flames emerge.

When Gonzalo returns to where he left his son he finds that Frank is gone. In the boy's place a baseball uniform lies above Fiona's burial ground. Gonzalo bends over to pick the jersey up. He holds it against his chest and sees it fits perfectly. He tries to rip it in half but the fabric won't tear. He sits on the ground and uses the shirt to drown out his sounds. Eventually he lowers the damp jersey before dropping it on top of the white baseball pants. For the first time since Fiona deteriorated to bone dust Gonzalo looks for the words he wrote to the corpse, but all he sees is the buildup of the boy's blood.

A Brief History of Running Away

Age Nine

The closest Gonzalo ever came to joining society was the first time he tried running away. When he went to sleep the night after his first etiquette lesson he had no plans of leaving the cemetery before morning. But while he snored under his sheets he had a series of vivid dreams that resulted in a cold sweat, and when he opened his eyes in the middle of the night he knew what he had to do. Gonzalo had to sneak into his parents' room and steal his great grandfather's shrunken head from the mantle above the fireplace. Once he slipped his father's favorite heirloom into his bag he left the funeral parlor.

Gonzalo entered the city as the sun began its ascent into the sky. He wandered through the windy streets, past the carnival mirror skyscrapers, unicyclist gangs and ballpark vendors until he saw a group of children standing on a corner. All the kids, who seemed to share Gonzalo's age, were wrapped in layers of colorful cloth. Gonzalo crept toward them, trying to blend in despite the black trench coat he was wearing and the spider web bag slung over his shoulder. Some of the kids glared at him, but for the most part they were too focused on themselves. Gonzalo tried to listen to their conversations, but he couldn't follow the action because he didn't know any of the names or shows or places or people they were talking about. Eventually a big yellow bus came, and the boy followed the crowd inside.

Gonzalo hid in the bathroom at the elementary school. He sat in the biggest stall staring at his great grandfather's head which he had taken out of his bag. It wasn't until the final bell rang and a flurry of girls entered the restroom that he gained the courage to enter the corridor. When he exited the stall the group of girls shrieked. When Gonzalo told them that it was okay, that he had gotten them a gift, and extended his great grandfather's shriveled head they screamed even louder. One of the girls, the prettiest of the group with her pink and blue pigtails, kept on shouting, "FREAK-A-ZOID," pointing at Gonzalo with both pointer fingers, looking from friend to friend as if she were asking them whether or not they were seeing what she saw. She didn't stop the name-calling until she fainted. As she hit the bathroom floor a few teachers stormed in, saving the rest of the girls from Gonzalo. They dragged the boy by his ears out of the girl's restroom and into the principal's office where it was discovered that he didn't attend the school. As a result the teachers threw him into the throes of society.

Hungry and homeless, Gonzalo once again wandered through the streets. He kept walking until he stumbled upon a massive park where kids of all ages created their own cacophonous webs. Gonzalo joined them in the park, forgetting his appetite and adding his own sounds to the patchy parade. Long after all the other kids went home, when the crescent moon began its ascent into the sky, a police officer found Gonzalo, who was still working on his web. The police officer escorted the boy back to the funeral parlor.

AGE TEN

onzalo tried to escape the cemetery again after the lashing of his lifetime. Sure, he'd received severe beatings in the past, especially—after he returned to the funeral parlor after his first attempt at running away and after he'd failed his etiquette examination—but neither of those compared to this whipping. Gonzalo's father slammed his son onto the floor before he beat the boy with coffin wood.

The wood first struck Gonzalo's heels, smashing his toes into the patio floor. Gonzalo's father then repeated the motion of lifting the wood above his head before sending it back down, this time battering the bottom of the boy's Achilles tendons. Again the man raised the whip, and again he brought it down, this time warring with Gonzalo's calves. Slowly the man made his way up his son's body, beating each inch of flesh as he went.

The man started with his son's feet because if he were to hit the head first the boy would be knocked senseless and would have only felt few of the remaining thirty-eight blows. By starting with the heels, it wasn't until the thirty-seventh beating that the coffin wood finally banged against the boy's head.

Thirty-seven was abrupt, shocking the boy's body out of the temporal numbness it had succumbed to. Thirty-eight caused blood to drip from Gonzalo's

121

ears. Thirty-nine sent the mind of the man's son into space. There was no forty. Forty would have turned Gonzalo into a corpse.

The first thing Gonzalo felt when he came to consciousness was impossible pain. A few seconds later the memories began to spawn. Once they settled the adrenaline attacked.

Gonzalo rose from the patio floor and ran into the funeral parlor. His legs limped uncontrollably, but they got him past the threshold. When he passed through the parlor he failed to see his family eating dinner; he failed to see them seeing him without concern. Though his family wasn't the only thing Gonzalo didn't realize after rising. He also missed that every contour of his body was covered in blood.

Whether it be the fault of adrenaline or not Gonzalo's negligence cost him the chance to escape. Roughly two blocks from the funeral parlor, the boy's energy evaporated, and pain consumed Gonzalo. Less than a minute after he stopped sprinting he collapsed unconscious.

If the boy had realized how much blood he lost, or how disfigured he looked maybe he would've realized that he'd never make it far. If only the adrenaline had left enough sense in the son to let him see that his family didn't digress from their dinner to keep him in the house, then maybe he could have foreseen what would come next. But of course the adrenaline didn't comply. In the end it was the black haired, baby blue-eyed deliveryman who lifted the nearly dead red Gonzalo off the ground and into the *Hole Foods*hearse on his way to the funeral parlor.

Earlier that day Gonzalo had been caught sneaking into the game room to watch television. The coffin wood came into play after he had apologized for breaking the boundaries.

AGE THIRTEEN

It took two weeks for Gonzalo to recover from the coffin wood whipping. As he rested in bed each day his desire to leave his family and their cemetery multiplied. Once he could return to the corpses in the graveyard he knew he couldn't just wait around for the next forty minus one. Once he could return to Mr. Oatsplash he knew he had to create the best escape plan ever. The plan would involve framing his sisters. He just couldn't paste the pieces together yet.

After three years of patient plotting with Mr. Oatsplash, though, he had polished his plan to perfection. True, the old corpse had told him time and time again that even if the plan succeeded he still wouldn't be able to leave, that he wouldn't be able to blend in with society, but Mr. Oatsplash was always saying depressing shit like that. And besides there was absolutely no fucking way he was actually going to wait around for his father to beat his body with coffin wood again. Gonzalo was thirteen and he knew his plan would work.

The plan: Gonzalo's twin sisters were always fighting with each other. When they weren't screaming they were pulling each other's hair, and when they weren't pulling hair they were biting each other's backs. His parents adored them and the loving malevolence they showed each other. They hardly hovered over the girls because they behaved the way they were trained. Gonzalo, on the other hand, constantly demanded their attention with the stuff he would say. So to distract his parents from punishing him Gonzalo planned to frame his sisters. At first he wanted to dig out a pit, fill it with snakes, cover it with a tarp, cover the tarp with grass and somehow get his sisters to walk over the tarp so they'd fall into the pit. Mr. Oatsplash said this was a good start, but that in the end this plan would only make his parents' proud. The old corpse said that if the boy truly wanted to distract his parents he'd have to frame his sisters with fondness. Gonzalo hadn't thought of that before, but the instant Mr. Oatsplash said it he knew it was the secret ingredient his plan needed. Gonzalo knew he'd have to compliment his sisters. This would undoubtedly convince them to chase him, and through the chase he'd get them to run over the tarp covering the pit, which would contain a plastic tea table stocked with crumpets, tea and Design-A-Dogs all dressed in princess attire. To top it all off Gonzalo would place a stereo under the tea table, and once his sisters landed on top of the table their combined weight would press the plastic against the sound system, playing the premade playlist compiled by Gonzalo, blasting music throughout the cemetery that would only be appropriate for a princess-themed tea party.

The plan worked wonderfully. Gonzalo told his sisters that they'd make pretty princesses, adding that they should be the first two princesses of the cemetery, and they became livid. They chased him around the graveyard until they fell through the ground. As the twins realized they'd fallen into a trap Gonzalo made a break for the front door of the funeral parlor. The last thing Gonzalo heard before he left home was his parents' voices scolding his sisters for playing such atrocious music and for playing with such abominable toys.

The problem with Gonzalo's supposedly perfect plan had nothing to do with his escape. The problem was that once Gonzalo reached the city his plan had already ended. He had no more moves to make. He had to think in the moment and that led him to rely on his sociability. But no matter how far he walked or how many strangers he forced into conversation, he couldn't get them to invite him to live with them. Even when he strongly hinted that they invite him over for the rest of their lives, they didn't ask the big question. As the sun started to set Mr. Oatsplash's negativity began to work its way into Gonzalo's conversations, and before the sun sank below the tops of the trees he found himself back beside the old corpse's coffin, demanding Mr. Oatsplash explain to him what he was doing to keep himself from connecting with society.

How To Become The Mortuary Monster

onzalo accepted the idea of murdering his parents when he was fifteen, though the idea itself had been resurfacing since he was six and first met Mr. Oatsplash. Mentally seeing society through Mr. Oatsplash's eyes brought desire to Gonzalo's heart, and with that came the motive to murder. But two years of plotting preceded the killing, and on his seventeenth birthday the conclusion came.

By the time Gonzalo turned seventeen his parents no longer knew the date they birthed their boy. Or if they did they didn't share the knowledge. As a result if killing wasn't on Gonzalo's mind he would have woken up as equally depressed and sleep deprived as he had on his sixteenth birthday, his fifteenth birthday and his fourteenth birthday which was the first one his parents had forgot. Then again, waking up in order to murder his family had made him smile, so he was probably depressed and sleep deprived all the same. Either way Gonzalo believed he was happy, and as he walked out of his room and then the funeral parlor before entering the cemetery to find Mr. Oatsplash he whistled. His steps were small skips. Out in the graveyard Gonzalo and Frank Arthur Oatsplash quickly reviewed the plan one last time, and once their conversation came to a close they put their last two years into action.

Mr. Oatsplash dived beneath the soil, and before the boy could finish picking his nose the corpse resurfaced with Gonzalo's gallery of art. Once the art was out and the color cut through the early morning haze, all they had to do was hide until Gonzalo's family arrived. And one by one they came.

Gonzalo's father fell first. The man stopped at the site of Gonzalo's painting, *Mortician Piss*, which consisted of a mixture of colors that from the distance of the funeral parlor depicted the son of the cemetery standing over his father's open grave and peeing onto the corpse inside. The man bent over to try and figure out how the blurring of colors on coffin wood could create such a monstrous mirage. Before the man could get a good look at how the colors coalesced Gonzalo swung his hatchet just above his father's shoe. The axe sliced the meat between the man's ankle and calf as if it were cloth, and the man screamed as his stump hit the ground. Before he could see his son he passed out from the pain. Once the man fell unconscious Mr. Oatsplash rose from his coffin to tourniquet the man's calf and to tie him to his tombstone. When that was finished Mr. Oatsplash returned to his coffin and Gonzalo found another spot to hide.

Emily, Gonzalo's mother, fell next. The painting that drew her into the gallery was *Corpsellatio*, which from afar featured a vertical view of Emily kneeling on the edge of a dugout grave, leaning into an open coffin, and sucking the climax out of a corpse. The painting's colors began to blur together as she approached, and she thought, *I've never fellated a corpse like that.*But, just like the artwork's distinctive features, her thoughts became nearly nonexistent as she noticed her unconscious husband tied to a tombstone. Gonzalo watched his mother knock her knuckles against his father's head, trying to wake him up. He crept toward them as his father slurred soft sounds and his mother sighed relief, realizing he was still alive. But her sigh was cut short when Gonzalo slammed down the axe on her foot, severing off everything past the heel. Without a sole to stand on Emily fell on top of her husband as the cemetery became black. When Emily's eyes blinked open again, she was tied to the tombstone beside her husband.

Mildred and Miranda were the last to fall. They, too, were drawn into the gallery by a particular painting. But unlike their mother they never took their eyes off the color, even after the image became incomprehensible. Because what they had seen was branded into their brains. As the painting blurred its projected image with its color integration they still saw themselves on all fours with Design-A-Dog heads and tails, chasing each other around a tea table and sniffing each other's anal glands. They still saw the painting Gonzalo calls *The Dance of the Dog*. Mildred and Miranda felt ill like they had the flu. The sensation of sickness the painting had implanted left their bodies when Gonzalo hit a two-run homerun, swinging the hatchet through the left knee of one twin and the right knee of the next in a single motion. The sisters screamed before they collapsed into silence.

Gonzalo dumped water on the heads of his tied up parents and sisters for the hundredth time, hoping they would come to consciousness. Finally they did, and Gonzalo's smile returned. "Father, mother, sisters, so long I have waited for this moment—"

"Two years to be exact," Mr. Oatsplash said, rising from the grave.

129

"Shut up, Frank," Gonzalo said. He regained his composure. "Two years I have waited for this moment. Two years I have planned for this. And finally, tonight, I'll be able to return what you have given me, Dad. And Mother, Mildred, Miranda, you're here because you laughed every time father whipped me. Even when I got thirty-nine lashings you laughed. Who's laughing now?" Gonzalo swung the axe into Mildred's thigh and laughed.

After swinging the axe into Mildred thirty-eight more times, Gonzalo moved onto Miranda. Miranda's voice vanished and her tear ducts dried while her brother cut up Mildred, so when the hatchet whistled toward her all she could do was shake. The shaking stopped when the axe struck, cutting off her remaining foot. She never shook again.

When he finished playing with his sisters Gonzalo prepared to strike his mother. Halfway through his swing he realized his mother had fainted again. He stopped the hatchet an inch from her hip and thought about dumping more water on her, but fuck it. He reeled back the axe before slinging it into his mother's side.

Then Gonzalo stepped in front of his father. The man sat there silently, staring into his son's eyes. Eventually the muscles on the man's face matched those of his son.

"Why're you smiling?" Gonzalo said. "Your wife's gone. Your favorite children are gone. And you're about to join them."

"It's just," the man said, silent tears drooping from the corners of his eyes, "I've never been so proud of you."

The hatchet fell from Gonzalo's hand. As he processed the meaning of the man's words, he reached down to retrieve his axe. Once the weapon was back in his hand he heard his corpse mother and corpse sisters echoing his father's sentiments. Together they told Gonzalo that they never thought they'd see the day when he'd become the Mortuary Monster, and now that they had they knew that all the pain they put him through had finally paid off. When Gonzalo returned his focus to his father he saw tears of joy plummeting from the man's eyes. He couldn't take it anymore. Instead of striking his father in the genitals like Gonzalo had planned, the hatchet hit the man's neck, hacking off his head.

Blood spurted out of Gonzalo's father, painting the rest of the boy's body red. Once the blood left the man his corpse head reappeared above his neck, uniting the father with the rest of his corpse family. Then, with the help of Mr. Oatsplash—who had waited in his coffin for the entirety of the killings— Gonzalo carried each member of his family, one by one, to the graves he had prepared for them. After Gonzalo and Mr. Oatsplash had tossed each corpse into its coffin the caretaker turned the key in the tombstone. His sisters, his mother and then his father were the first four coffins Gonzalo had ever closed.

After locking away his family Gonzalo had Frank Arthur Oatsplash help him track down every corpse in the cemetery. They beat the corpses unconscious, carried them to their gravesites and then Gonzalo closed them in their coffins. Eventually all the corpses were gone; Frank Arthur Oatsplash and Gonzalo were the last two people, dead and alive, in the cemetery.

After a minute of eyeing each other, Gonzalo started the last conversation they would ever have by reassuring himself. "It's too late to turn back now," he said.

"It's never too late, child," Mr. Oatsplash said, standing in his coffin, refusing to satisfy the Mortuary Monster before him.

Gonzalo explained to Frank Arthur Oatsplash that he was wrong. It wasn't long before he twisted the key in the corpse's tombstone, forever closing the only friendship he ever had.

It hits Gonzalo like a heart attack. Frank left him alone in the cemetery seven years ago, and it just now hits him. Gonzalo looks into the mirror and knowingly sees the monster he vowed he would never become.

Gonzalo almost laughs. Instead, as he stares into his eyes, he cries. His entire existence he has questioned himself and his inability to join society. He knew he never belonged outside of the cemetery but he could never understand why and it drove him mad. Gonzalo thinks about the disdain he had for his son, about the distance he put between them by forcing the boy to play baseball. He thinks about the hatred he held for Frank, the hatred he had when he learned about Frank's love of fashion and the hatred he had once he realized the boy was never coming back to the cemetery. He thinks about past thoughts, hears himself cursing Frank, the goddamn half-corpse, for being able to do what he has never done. But now he finally understands why.

Gonzalo's fist approaches its reflection, shattering the glass into shards. Slivers shine out from under his knuckles before beadlets of blood slowly mask the light. Gonzalo still stares at the wall where his reflection used to be, mentally rearranging his appearance so that it fits the image of his father. As he licks the blood from his hand, though, his father evaporates from his head, and he sees himself without a cover, finally conscious of unfiltered guilt. For the first time in his life Gonzalo is ly aware that the monster of his childhood cannot compare to the one he has become.

How To Kill The Mortuary Monster

$\mathcal{M}$r. Oatsplash once said to Gonzalo that he would know when he was ready to leave the cemetery because he'll no longer belong. At the time Gonzalo thought Mr. Oatsplash was talking out of his ass. Gonzalo thought most of what the corpse said came through his entropic ass. But after waking up this afternoon Gonzalo finally understands what Mr. Oatsplash had meant.

Yesterday, when he first came across his guilt, the only other thing he felt was regret. He regretted not taking Mr. Oatsplash's words seriously, especially after he had killed his family. Thoughts about the amount of time and trouble he could have saved if he had only listened began to surface, but after a few minutes he forced himself to ignore them because they made him feel significantly worse. He shrugged them off, telling himself he was just a boy then and that it was only natural for him to ignore Mr. Oatsplash's advice. But what he couldn't shrug off is the killing of his family and closing the coffins of all the corpses he loved—Mr. Oatsplash, Vincent and Victoria, Lionel, Henry and most of all, the killing of

Fiona.

Gonzalo regretted that he never kept his promise to Fiona. The one he made the week before she became bone dust. Gonzalo had promised her that they'd raise their coming child together as equal parts of a family whole. She believed him, and he even believed himself. Despite the shock of seeing his son for the first time, once he was out, Gonzalo knew he meant every word of his promise. Of course Fiona had to become the first corpse to die. Gonzalo regretted that after realizing Fiona had passed, he didn't keep his promise to her for Frank's sake but instead allowed it to wither with the bones of the boy's mother.

Gonzalo hardly slept the previous night. The regrets kept building on themselves like the dead during wartime. One regret led to another and another until he'd downed enough Long Island Iced Tea to last him a hundred parties. Seconds before the liquor sent him to sleep he had one last thought. Technically, in a backwards and fucked up sort of way, he told himself he kept the most important promise of all: he got his son away from the cemetery. The thought didn't make him feel any better.

Besides having the hangover of the cemetery century, when Gonzalo wakes up this afternoon he feels completely out of place. It takes some time, but after an hour or two Gonzalo recalls the words of his only childhood friend. With this recollection comes another realization: Gonzalo no longer belongs in the cemetery.

This knowledge doesn't make him feel any better. Instead it makes him feel infinitely worse. Gonzalo always thought that the day he knew he belonged in society would be the happiest moment of his life. He never imagined that it would make him aware of how strongly he didn't deserve to go.

Gonzalo knows he's the Mortuary Monster, and even though he can now act his way through society convincing everyone he is one of them, deep down, Gonzalo will always know the cemetery is his home. After this thought, for the first time since yesterday, the guilt starts to subside. Gonzalo has finally seen himself from afar. No matter how closely he sees himself again, blurring the reality of who he is with his ideal self, the image from afar has branded itself into his brain. Gonzalo will always see himself as nothing more than the Mortuary Monster.

He knows what he has to do. He has never been more confident about anything his entire life. The only way he can conceive the thought of living with himself is to embody the corpses he spent his whole life trying to leave behind. Gonzalo grabs a rope from the funeral parlor, ties it to the wooden beam above his bed and tries to jump onto the floor. His toes never touch, and eventually his body comes back a corpse.

PART THREE
AFTERLIFE

PART THREE

APPENDIX

THE VISITORS

Gonzalo has been hanging from the beam in his bedroom for three weeks now. He could have untied himself, but he didn't see the point. Without the hope of joining society Gonzalo would have nothing to do. At least this way he has untying himself to look forward to when the boredom overcomes the guilt. Besides, being stuck in a noose grants him time to reflect on his life and what he could have done to save his friendships with his favorite corpses, Mr. Oatsplash and Fiona. When his solitude and sleep deprivation start to drive him insane he even thinks of ways he could have helped save his relationship with his parents and sisters. But mostly Gonzalo spends his time gathering the courage to think about Frank and every instance of parenting that he could have changed to preserve their relationship and to prevent himself from becoming a bigger Mortuary Monster than his father. That's what he is doing when he hears the knock on the front door of the funeral parlor. Thinking about how he should have spent less time indoctrinating his son with baseball and more time generating his own passion for his son's increasing interest in fashion.

Gonzalo reaches for the rope tied tightly around

his neck and pulls it as far from his throat as possible. "Coming," he says once the noose is loose enough to let him speak. Gonzalo starts to swing his body back and forth until he has enough force to flip himself onto the beam where he begins to untie the rope. When he is free from the beam Gonzalo is able to untie the rope from his neck. He tilts his head to both sides, using his hands to help the bone crack, sending sound through the funeral parlor and causing the crows on the patio to fly away. Gonzalo gets off the beam and goes to the front door to let in his guests.

If Gonzalo hadn't hung himself and spent every moment since growing increasingly mad as he traveled through his life's vast variety of flaws, he probably would have been more hesitant to see who is knocking on his door. A year after Frank left the cemetery the deliveryman had begun dropping the groceries off on the front porch instead of knocking. Gonzalo hasn't seen a single being, dead or alive, for years. Despite his lack of company Gonzalo doesn't think twice about who would be visiting. His obsession with his past has enabled him to believe that the knock is just another family here to deposit their deceased. His corpse hand clutches the knob, and the door creaks.

No sound comes from either side of the door once it has opened. Gonzalo thinks what he sees merely confirms his suspicion that he has already gone mad. There cannot actually be anyone on the other side of the door because what he sees is a grownup version of his son wearing a baseball uniform like the one he had Frank create as a child. The only difference is the color. In the center of this jersey is a big blue baseball with orange stitching, and inside the ball is an orange illustration of the funeral parlor. Next to Frank stands his wife, and between them is their one-forth corpse daughter, who seems to have only inherited hollow eyes from her father. Gonzalo almost utters that the family before him and their uniforms are beautiful, but he stops himself because he is afraid that if he speaks, or even moves, the vision will evaporate.

On the other side of the door Frank doesn't move a muscle because he is still shocked to be standing in front of his corpse father even though he knew what he would find after he knocked. His wife and their child follow his lead. After a few minutes of silence Frank finally says, "Hi, Dad."

Hearing his son's voice brings Gonzalo out of what he believed to be a hallucinatory trance. Slowly he extends his right wrist toward his son, lightly touching the tips of his fingers to Frank's cheek. After feeling the face before him, Gonzalo breaks down. Tears drip down his decayed face for a couple minutes. After that he regains a sense of composure and says in a voice barely above a whisper, "You . . . you're real."

"I am real," Frank says, wrapping his arms around his father, reassuring the reality with physicality.

Gonzalo gives into his desire and returns his son's hug, but after a few seconds he steps away from Frank. "I'm sorry," he says. "It's just . . . Won't you come in for some tea?"

Frank nods and his family follows his father into the funeral parlor.

Gonzalo grabs a pitcher and pours four Long Island Iced Teas. He hands a glass to each of his guests and goes to sit down. Before he gets to his seat Frank says, "Goz is too young to drink this."

"Excuse me?" Gonzalo says.

"Our daughter can't drink this," Frank says. "She's only three. You have any milk?"

"Of course," Gonzalo says. He grabs the glass from the girl and replaces it with milk. Once he sits down he quietly says, "Her name is Goz?"

"Yes," Frank says. "We named her Goz." To his daughter: "Goz, won't you say hello to your grandpa?"

Goz looks at her mother, shielding her face from Gonzalo with her hand. Her mother gives her a look that says to go on, and she peeks over her fingertips. "Hi," she says into her palm.

"Hello" Gonzalo says, mimicking her shyness in the form of tears.

"And this here," Frank says, wrapping his arm around the woman beside him, "is my wife Clementine."

"It's good to finally meet you," she says. "I've heard so much about you."

Gonzalo just nods his head, ashamed by whatever it is she knows about him.

"Frank here," she goes on, "as well as my father, have told me so many great things."

Gonzalo shakes his head. "It's good to meet you, too," he finally says. Then, "It's great to see all of you. I just . . ." His tear ducts start to sweat. "I'm sorry. I just don't understand."

"Maybe this will help," Frank says. "I forgive you."

"How can you?" Gonzalo says before his son can say anything else.

"Because I know so much now that I never knew before. I understand so much more."

Frank waits for Gonzalo to say something but a minute of silence passes. Rising from the table Frank continues, "I'll explain out on the patio. But first let me get you another drink." Frank grabs Gonzalo's empty glass from the table and replaces it with the drink that was intended for Goz. Then he refills his and his wife's glasses with more Long Island Iced Tea before getting another milk for his daughter. "After you," he says to the corpse, and Gonzalo leads the party out to the patio.

Once they have all seated themselves at the table

and Gonzalo has gotten the fire pit going, Frank clears his throat. "I guess I'll start with right after I left the cemetery."

Gonzalo takes a long sip of tea and lights a cigar. After he inhales he nods his head.

"When you found me in the closed side of the cemetery and took away all my fabric," Frank says, "I fully realized for the first time how much I hated you. I knew that the fabric was the only thing keeping me remotely happy, and once you had taken it there was no reason for me to stay in the funeral parlor. I didn't care what happened, if I died or never found another friend outside of the cemetery, because I knew nothing could possibly be worse than living here.

"And that's how the first few days went. After I left the cemetery I got lost in the woods. I couldn't find any water, and although I discovered some berries my thirst was literally killing me. The last thing I remember from the forest is that I was again aimlessly walking, my third or fourth day, I don't really know, hoping to find a stream or a lake or any source of water. At one point I stumbled across a road, and as I reached it I passed out. The next thing I knew I was in the back of a car and someone was pouring water into my mouth. After drinking as much water as my body could handle, I fell asleep.

"I slept for fifteen hours, and when I woke up I was completely confused. I had no idea where I was and no memory of the last few days. But after a few minutes of freaking out, hunger overcame my anxiety. And then, right as my stomach began to growl, I saw a girl for the first time in my life." Frank pauses his story to shoot his wife a smile. "She walked into the room with a plate full of food and told me her name was Clementine. Then she left and said she'd be back for the dishes after I finished my breakfast. I scarfed down the eggs and the pancakes and the toast and the fruit in no more than ten minutes. It was the most satisfying meal I had ever had. When Clementine returned to get the dishes I asked her where I was.

"She left without answering my question and my anxiety returned. A minute later she came back with her father. And you'll never believe who he was," Frank says.

Gonzalo is in the process of lighting a second cigar, and it takes him a moment to realize Frank is waiting for some sort of response. After the first hit he exhales. "Who?"

"The deliveryman," Frank says, a smile spreading across his face. "Apparently he found me unconscious on the roadside as he made his way to the funeral parlor to deliver a month's worth of groceries to you. He told me I was the second child he found on that road, and that the first time he brought the kid back to the funeral parlor. He said he couldn't make the biggest mistake of his life twice, so he brought me back to his house in the city to raise me as his own son.

"Over the next few months the deliveryman, whose name was Jeremy by the way, became incredibly ill. Unfortunately his illness never left him, and a year after he found me he passed. But despite his illness, during the last year of his life, he taught me how to drive. Once he was gone I took over his house and the *Hole Foods* business. Each month I delivered your groceries. I was afraid of what would happen if we saw each other, though, so I just dropped them off on the front porch. But by this point I had already forgiven you. I came by at least once a week to watch you through the windows, hoping change would come.

"The reason I was able to deliver your groceries to you—to forgive you—is because of what Jeremy told me before he died. Besides teaching me the ins and outs of the *Hole Foods* business, he also told me about your childhood. He told me that when my father was young, he found him once unconscious on the side of the road, covered in blood and barely breathing. He told me that when he carried you to your parents, handing you over to your father, all the mortician said was, 'Is this all you brought or did you bring us our groceries like we pay you to?' Jeremy told me your father then tossed you onto the floor, and nobody acted like anything was wrong. After that Jeremy said he started paying attention to you whenever he dropped off the groceries, and each month he realized that a few new bruises appeared on your body.

"I forgave you right after I learned about your childhood. I understood why you were the way you are—"

"That doesn't excuse anything," Gonzalo interrupts. "The things I did to you, to everyone." Gonzalo takes a hard hit from his cigar.

"Maybe not for you," Frank says. "But for me it made a difference. It showed me that you didn't know how to love, that you didn't know how to raise a child. It showed me that you did everything you knew, that you wanted what was best for me, to be normal enough to join society like you never could.

"Don't get me wrong, you were the worst fucking parent I have ever encountered, but knowing your childhood helped me look past your flaws and see what you wanted to be for me. And because of that I forgive you."

"I never asked to be forgiven," Gonzalo says. "You can't forgive me."

"I can and I have, a long time ago," Frank says. "And when I saw your body hanging from the beam through your bedroom window, I knew I needed to see you again.

"That's why, Dad," Frank says, setting his hand on

his corpse father's femur, "my family and I have returned to the cemetery to be your caretaker."

It takes a minute for Gonzalo to understand the weight of his son's words. Before he can respond Frank adds, "Gonzalo, we want to be your caretaker. My wife and I have talked it over, and we want to start fresh. We want a relationship with you. You're the only family we have left, and we want to be close to you. Besides, this is the perfect place to create my first collection of clothes, *Cloth from the Crypt.*"

"I'm so thankful you've come," Gonzalo says. He pauses to pass smoke through his rib cage. "Seeing you again, meeting your wife and my beautiful granddaughter, is the best thing that has ever happened to me. I love all of you more than you can imagine." Gonzalo pauses and looks out at the cemetery. He sees memories of him and his son, sees the misunderstanding and the hatred on both his and the boy's face. He says, "But you can't be my caretaker. This far from the city, your clothing line will fail. I spent your whole life trying to keep a promise, and now that I've finally done it I won't let you come back here to keep me from keeping the only promise I've ever kept."

"I want to be here," Frank says. "I want to take care of you."

"I would never be able to live with myself if you came back to the cemetery," Gonzalo says. "I need you to understand this. I mean, look at this place." Gonzalo uses his arms to gesture toward the decaying wall which no longer keeps the color on the closed side of the cemetery.

Frank nods his head and finishes his drink. He says he understands.

"Is there anything we can do for you, Gonzalo?" Clementine asks

"Yes," Gonzalo says. "Before you leave, I need you to make me a promise."

"Anything," Frank says.

"I need you to close my coffin. I've locked so many corpses in their coffins while I was alive, and now it's my turn." Gonzalo takes the last drag from his cigar and lets it fall to the floor.

Frank finishes his wife's drink. He walks inside, grabs the pitcher from the fridge and comes back to the patio. He downs the half-full pitcher. "I'll do anything," he says again.

Gonzalo leads Frank, Clementine and Goz out to his grave. When they arrive Gonzalo hugs his son and daughter-in-law. Then he holds his granddaughter. He tells Goz that he loves her and that her father will be a wonderful dad. And then, with admiration in his eyes, he says, "Son, I'm just so proud of you."

"I love you, dad," Frank says, his eyes becoming clouds as he withholds tears.

Gonzalo dives beneath the ground and enters his tombstone. A minute later he hears the key enter the lock, but before it turns he rises one last time.

"Wait!" Gonzalo says.

"What?" Franks says, hopeful.

"Can I . . ." Gonzalo points at his son's chest. "Can I take your uniform with me? To remember."

Frank takes off his uniform and hands it to his father before the corpse can blink. Clementine hands him a picture of their family. Gonzalo inhales his son's scent from the jersey, and tears wrinkle his vision as he looks at the photograph. Again Gonzalo goes underground.

In his coffin Gonzalo straightens out the uniform and places the picture above the head-hole. As he wraps his arms around the place where his son's presence was, Frank twists the key. Gonzalo hears his coffin close.

THE END

ABOUT THE AUTHOR

If Andrew J. Stone were a corpse, he'd be buried in a mushroom suit. If he were a superhero, he'd be Marx. If he were to have a cat, her name would be Alice, and he'd be living in an apartment that allowed pets. His work has appeared in Hobart, Gutter Eloquence, New Dead Families, Drunk Monkeys, Red Fez, and DOGZPLOT, among other places, and The Mortuary Monster is his first book. He lives in Hawthorne, California with his wife and their many bills.